Why Does
the Coquí
Sing?

Why Does the Coquí Sing?

by Barbara Garland Polikoff

Holiday House / New York

1   3   5   7   9   10   8   6   4   2

Library of Congress Cataloging-in-Publication Data

Polikoff, Barbara Garland.
Why does the coqui sing? / by Barbara Garland Polikoff.—1st ed.
        p.   cm.
Summary: When thirteen-year-old Luz and her family move from Chicago
to her stepfather's native home of Puerto Rico, she and her brother Rome
struggle to adjust and to decide where it is they really belong.
ISBN 0-8234-1817-0 (hardcover)
1. Puerto Ricans—Juvenile fiction. [1. Puerto Ricans—Fiction.
2. Moving, Household—Fiction. 3. Family life—Puerto Rico—Fiction.
4. Puerto Rico—Fiction. 5. Identity—Fiction.] I. Title.
PZ7.P75284Wh 2004
[Fic]—dc22
2003056776

For María Velasquez and
all my Puerto Rican students who helped me
hear the song of the coquí.

To the memory of
Jane Jordan Browne

Contents

How Could Home Be
a Place I've Never Seen?

I'm in Puerto Rico. Just where I *don't* want to be. Me, Luz Sorrento; Mami; my stepfather, Leon; my little sister, Marisol; and my sixteen-year-old brother, Rome. (Rome is short for Romance—can you believe Mami named a boy Romance?)

Leon is trying to flag down a taxi, but they're all filled and race right by.

Mami lifts her face to the hot blue sky. "Can you believe we were in freezing Chicago this morning? Feel that sun!"

Leon bought her a yellow orchid in the airport, and she's pushed her hair back and pinned the orchid behind her ear. She looks beautiful.

I look awful. When things are okay in my life, I don't look so bad, but I can never look really great. I have dark eyes and long black hair like Mami's, but my face is rounder than hers, and here's the worst part—I have a scar running from my left ear down to my jaw, stopping right where my chin begins. I got it when Rome was mad at me for waking him up on his one morning to sleep late. He had jumped out of bed and chased me, growling like a monster. Trying to get away, I tripped and cut myself on the glass coffee table.

At first I was proud of the scar. I was only six years old and I liked all the attention. I was nine when I stared at myself in the mirror one day and realized how much it looked like a worm. I stormed out of the bathroom and started yelling, "Rome, you ruined my face! I hate you!"

Mami said that I should try to forgive Rome. He didn't mean to make me fall. It was just bad luck. I looked up at the stars that night and said, "I forgive you, Rome," ten times, slowly. But then he'd do something to upset me and I would scream at him so hard, I knew I was still screaming about the scar.

Mami says it will fade as I get older. I'm thirteen now and it still looks as pink and wormy as ever. Mami and I are saving up so I can have an operation to erase it. By the time we have enough money I may be a creaky old lady.

"Taxi!" Leon yells, jumping off the curb and waving at an empty cab. The cabdriver jerks to a stop and Leon whips open the back door for Mami before he and the cabdriver stuff our luggage into the trunk. His smile is so big, it almost falls off his face. He and Mami have been married for almost a year, and he still looks goo-goo-eyed at her. Rome says it makes him want to throw up.

Poor Rome. For three years he had been hoping we'd hear a saxophone playing "When the Saints Come Marching In" outside our window. The next minute our dad would open the door and dance into the living room, and he and Mami would be together again. When Mami married Leon, that dream died.

Marisol pushes into the taxi to get the window seat. She's not even five, so she can push in anywhere. Her hair is tied with pink bows into two fat ponytails that stick out on either side of her head. She's cute but pesty. Mami moves in close to her so that either Rome or I can get the other window seat. Rome's so miserable about leaving Chicago, he couldn't care less, so I take it. He was a star on the hockey team, plus he had just gotten his first steady girlfriend. I guess it's hard giving up being popular. I wouldn't know.

"See all the calm trees!" Marisol says excitedly.

3

Mami laughs. "*Palm* trees, Marisol. They're beautiful, aren't they?"

I stare at the trees. "They're ugly. All those dead leaves hanging down like dirty underwear." I'm thinking about the beautiful evergreens outside our apartment in Chicago. On Christmas all the neighbors would get together and decorate them with hundreds of tiny white lights.

Mami's too happy to let my grumpiness bother her. I keep on yakking. "Palm trees would sure look stupid decorated with Christmas lights."

Marisol grabs Mami's hand. "We're going to have a Christmas tree in Puerto Rico, aren't we, Mami?"

"Yeah," says Rome, pulling one of her ponytails. "And Santa's going to wear a bathing suit and ride in on a surfboard."

Marisol glowers at Rome. "He is not!"

"It's September and all the trees are a boring green," I say, bouncing the ball into Rome's court. We do this sometimes—play "talk tennis." It's usually designed to drive Mami nuts.

Rome sends the ball flying back. "The trees in Puerto Rico are too dumb to change color."

Leon twists around in his seat so he can see us. "When I still lived in Puerto Rico, a woman sitting on a park bench had a coconut fall on her head. So now all of the coconut palms in public places have their coconuts removed."

Leon must be feeling good. Usually he doesn't say much. He was Mami's student in Chicago, where she taught English as a Second Language. I guess you would say he's good-looking. He's taller than most Puerto Rican men with eyes as black as olives and a sharply carved nose and mouth. (He has Indian blood from his ancestors.) I thought that if Mami ever married again, I would have something to say about who my stepfather would be. It didn't work that way. She fell for Leon and that was that.

Leon's thirty-six, three years younger than Mami. That's a lot. The night she gave me the news that they were getting married, I burst out, "But he's so much younger than you!"

She smiled and kissed me on the nose. "It is not how many years you live that's important, Luz, but what you do with them."

I shot back, "What's Leon done with his years that's so great?"

The happiness in Mami's eyes shut down. I had hurt her more than I meant to. "It's just that Leon's so quiet."

"I love Leon's quietness." Mami's voice changed from soft to starched. "Leon talks when he has something to say."

I knew Mami was thinking—*not like your father.* My father was a *big* talker. He played saxophone in a band, so he was used to performing. Mami said the trouble was that he never stopped performing. I felt terrible that they were quarreling right before he left to play in Italy with his band. He was happy about going because he still had family living in Rome, where he was born. He and Mami went there for their honeymoon. That's how Rome got his name, Rome and honeymoon equal romance. Mami gave me my name, Luz, meaning light. It's short and I like it.

My father stayed in Italy longer and longer. I wrote a letter telling him I missed him. Rome wrote two letters. Mami wrote hundreds of them. After he was away a year and a half, she got a divorce.

"Conci," Leon says. (Mami's real name is Constancia, which she hates.) "We're going to arrive at your sister's early."

"I'm counting the minutes!"

A bump in the road joggles us. Marisol catches the orchid that slips from Mami's hair and gives it to her.

Mami breathes in its sweet smell. "Leon, I'd like Luz to have a turn wearing the flower."

Leon nods. He loves flowers. He even talks to them—more than he talks to me. He worked as a super- visor in a big nursery that grew orchids. When he moved into our apartment, plants began sprouting all over the place, on windowsills, bookshelves, kitchen cabinets, even on the TV. Rome told our dog, Pepito, to watch out or Leon would plant his water dish.

Mami pins the flower in my hair with a bobby pin.

"Mami, I look stupid."

"You look pretty, doesn't she, Leon?"

I pull the flower out of my hair before Leon can answer and give it back to Mami.

She just holds it in her hand. I lean back against the seat. The easiest thing would be to fall asleep. Then I'd hear nothing, see nothing, and feel nothing.

Instead, my thoughts go to the day Mami first told me that we were going to move to Puerto Rico. I couldn't believe what I was hearing. My mouth turned so dry, the words stuck like fuzz on my tongue. "What did you say?"

Mami repeated that she and Leon had decided to move the family to Puerto Rico, where we would have a chance for a better, safer life. Leon was going to get a piece of land from the government and build a house for us and grow fruit and orchids to sell. No more living in a crowded, dangerous city where police sirens keep you awake at night and you worry if anyone you know has been shot.

"Luz," Mami had said, holding my eyes with hers. "I understand how upset you feel, but you'll make friends, do things, go places. And we'll be close to Tata, Tía Ana, and your cousin, Juanita. Pretty soon Puerto Rico will seem like home. It *is* your real home, you know."

"No, it's not! How could home be a place I've never seen?"

And Teresa isn't in Puerto Rico, I wanted to shout, or Marta or Shanti. My school, where I've gone since kindergarten and where the blue tile with the white horse that I made in art class is cemented in the wall, isn't in Puerto Rico. Or the cozy room in the church where we have our Wise Girls Club meetings.

"It's Leon's idea, I know it!" I said, fighting back tears. "You never talked about going back to Puerto Rico before you met him."

"I knew I wouldn't return on my own, Luz. So there was no sense talking about it." Mami put her arms around me, but I wriggled away. I felt like picking up my shoes, my book, a lamp, anything, and throwing it against the wall.

Words are like horses sometimes—they gallop through the door of your mouth even if you don't want them to. "And besides, it costs a lot to go to Puerto Rico. We'll have to use up all the money we've been saving for my operation."

"Luz . . . Luz, so that's what you're worried about."

Mami took my face and held it, speaking straight

into my teary eyes. "Luz, the money we saved for your operation will not be touched. And as soon as we're settled, I'll put dollars in your No-Scar Box whenever I can. I promise."

I pulled away. Even though I believed her, it didn't make me feel any better. The only thing that could do that would be her saying "Luz, I love you more than anything in the world. If it makes you unhappy to move to Puerto Rico, we won't go." And that wasn't going to happen.

I Hear the Coquí Sing

Riding in a car in San Juan is scarier than the worst roller coaster. No one pays attention to the speed limit. We're all jerked forward in our seats as our driver screeches to a halt so he won't slam into a car that ran a red light.

"Everyone in Puerto Rico must have flunked driver's ed," Rome grumbles.

I look through the car window to see this place that's supposed to be my home. The sidewalk is so crowded that you'd think it was Christmas. A girl in a short dress and bright makeup walks next to a tall woman wearing a long, flowered skirt, her straight black hair swinging like a curtain. Some men in suits, some in awful flowered shirts. The flowered shirts are probably tourists. Little kids drag along, holding their mothers' hands. An old woman in a straw hat and baggy men's pants pushes a stroller loaded with bulging plastic bags. There's a whole strip of expensive-looking stores with people going in and out of revolving doors. It's the same as State Street in Chicago. People who look rich walk fast, as if someone important is waiting for them. Poor people walk slowly, as if they're not eager to get where they're going. Chicago doesn't have stands with neat towers of shining fruit though. Or flower stalls on nearly every corner that catch your eye like neon lights flashing.

Mami says she would like to buy some flowers for Ana, but Leon thinks stopping is too dangerous.

"Drivers here think flashing lights are some kind of decoration," Rome says.

Mami frowns. "Rome, you have not said *one* positive thing since we left Chicago."

"But there—" Rome stops. Mami's still looking at him. He shrugs and slumps back into the seat.

It's even harder for Rome to leave Chicago than it is for me. He can't really believe our dad has forgotten him. He worries that if we've moved to Puerto Rico and our dad comes back, how would he ever find us? Rome loved being with our dad. He'd take him to a hockey or baseball game, sometimes to a band rehearsal. Mami knew I felt left out. "He's just more comfortable doing boy things," she said. "It's not because he doesn't love you as much as Rome." I didn't believe her. When he bought Rome a miniature silver saxophone, he gave me a package of Tootsie Rolls. They were stale and Mami wouldn't let me eat them because I might break my teeth.

"And that's the University of Puerto Rico," Mami says. We're passing sleek lawns and flowers and important-looking white buildings. A clock tower sticks high up over the trees. Marisol thinks it looks like a giant birdhouse.

We finally drive out of the busy part of town. I lean back. Stores are smaller and the road narrows. The driver speeds up around the curves instead of slowing down. Marisol topples into Mami's lap. My stomach turns somersaults.

I close my eyes, then open them to see that we're driving along a street with square cement houses jammed together and painted different colors.

"Mami, can we live in a pink house like that one?" Marisol hangs out of the window so far that Mami yanks her back in.

"We'll have to live in whatever color house Tía Ana picked for us."

"Why are all the houses made of cement?" I ask.

"Bugs chew up the wooden ones," Leon says.

Marisol shivers. "I hate bugs!"

I screw up my face. "Spiders grow as big as chickens here, Marisol. I'll get you a leash so you can take one for a walk."

"Luz!" Marisol leans across Mami and Rome, and punches me in the stomach. I squeal and roll my eyes and make her laugh. She punches me again, then waits for me to squeal and roll my eyes. I don't and she pouts.

I sit back in the seat and try to make the time go faster by thinking how great it will be to see Tata again. He isn't shriveled up and bent like a lot of old men. He's tall and has wide shoulders and stands very straight. His hair is white like corn silk and his skin is nut brown from always being in the sun. His hands have perfect white moons on each fingernail. Rome has those same perfect moons. I wish I had them.

Tata always came to visit us for three weeks in the summer. I'd wake in the morning feeling excited about something. Then I'd remember. Tata! I'd run down to the basement, where he'd be working on Marisol's and my dollhouse. It has a curving stairway and miniature furniture for every room. I loved to watch his strong fingers carve the tiny chairs and tables. He even carved a toilet with a lid you could lift. Last Christmas he sent us three beautiful figures he painted. They're called santos because they represent saints.

As we approach a sign, CALZADOS, Leon asks the driver to slow down. We drive past the town square with burnt grass and a water fountain sending a spurt of water dribbling over the rim. A small cream-colored dog is drinking from a puddle. He reminds me of Pepito. We had to leave him with Tía Luisa. I try not to let myself think about him. I'm tired of crying.

Stores lean away from the stores next to them like people who aren't happy to be close to each other. The Sun Café looks like the only place I'd want to go into. It has a yellow awning and a jungle of plants in the window.

The grocery store is small with an outside fruit stand that's half empty.

"I hope we can get what we need there," Mami says doubtfully.

"We'll have to, Conci," Leon says. "We may not have a car for a while."

Rome groans.

"I wonder if they even have a church here," I say.

"Sunday mornings Juanita picks Ana up," Mami answers, "and they drive to a church in San Juan."

"We can't go because we don't have a car." Rome ducks his head as if Mami is going to hit him.

In Chicago we didn't go to church regularly the way some of my friends did. Teresa called us EC Catholics because we went only on Easter and Christmas.

The biggest store we see is the Champas Furniture Store. It has two large windows filled with couches and chairs.

"I went to high school with Luis Champas," Leon says. "He took over the store when his uncle died. He may give us a discount."

"Do they have a library here?" I ask.

Rome smirks. "Library? What's that?"

He's being obnoxious. But it's better than having him half dead.

"From Top to Toe." Mami laughs. "You can get a haircut in that store and buy a pair of shoes."

"I hope not at the same time," Leon says.

Mami gets serious. "We're going to be in Calzados for a while. We better not make fun of it anymore."

That shuts us all up. I close my eyes and don't open them until Mami cries, "There's Ana. See! Standing by the house with the bougainvillea."

The driver pulls along the curb and Mami opens the door almost before the car has stopped. "Ana!" she cries, running into Tía Ana's outstretched arms. The two sisters hug each other and kiss and hug again. Marisol and I climb out of the car, and Tía Ana pounces on us and smothers us with hugs and a lot of little kisses.

"Kisses from Tata and a kiss from me," she says.

"But where's Tata?"

"You'll see Tata soon. The long ride tires him."

I'm so disappointed, I could cry. I need to see Tata that very moment to make coming to Puerto Rico bearable.

Rome's still slouched in the car. Tía Ana pulls him out and kisses him. The tips of his ears turn pink. Then it's Leon's turn. She shines a smile at him.

"Constancia is a lucky woman. Such good-looking men in her family."

Tía Ana could be almost as beautiful as Mami, but she's shorter and wider. Putting a belt on her would be like putting a belt on a gallon milk bottle. Her black hair is pulled back from her forehead and curled into a bun with a dragonfly pin stuck in it. She wears much more makeup than Mami. Even after blotting her lipstick on all of us her mouth is still tomato red.

"Come into the house! I've been chewing up my manicure waiting for you!"

Tía Ana's living room matches her. It's cheerful with fat furniture, a white couch, and a chair covered with a pattern of green leaves and pink flowers. A white plushy rug covers most of the black cement floor. Marisol burrows into it and purrs.

Tía Ana insists we're starved and waits impatiently while we wash up. There's only one small bathroom, so Leon and Rome wash at the kitchen sink.

We sit around a table covered with a pink plastic tablecloth that crackles. Tía Ana brings platters of pasteles, guanimes, pigeon peas, and a salad of corn, tomatoes, and yucca. She hovers over us and squeezes a chair in between Rome and me only after she serves a dessert of tembleque. She looks from Leon to Mami and back to Leon again. Her cheerfulness is gone.

"Ana, is anything wrong?" Mami asks.

"Can you believe it?" she bursts out. "I gave the people who were going to rent their house to you a month's rent and yesterday I got my check back! They're not moving! I grabbed the phone and told them they can't do that. We have a contract! They hung up on me." She seems close to tears. "I wanted everything to be so nice for you!"

Mami puts her arm around her. "We'll find another place, Ana. Don't worry."

"You'll stay at my house while you look. I can sleep at my friend's. Rome will have to sleep on the couch. I don't know what he'll do with his big feet."

Rome shrugs. "I'll unscrew them."

Tía Ana stares at him. Mami laughs. Tía Ana's not used to Rome's sense of humor.

Mami and Tía Ana talk the whole time we do dishes. They don't even stop to breathe.

"I'm really tired," I say. "Could someone please tell me where I should sleep?"

Tía Ana takes Marisol and me to Juanita's old bedroom. It has two beds with bright yellow spreads and a rocking chair with a stuffed koala bear sitting on it.

"That's Juanita's KoKo," Tía Ana says. "You can sleep with it if you like, Marisol." She kisses us good night and then blows another kiss as she walks out of the room.

"Tía Ana is very kissy," Marisol says. "Do you like her, Lula?"

"I like her a lot."

We change into our pajamas and brush our teeth. Holding KoKo, Marisol squeezes into bed with me and buries herself under the covers.

"Are you both settled?" Mami asks as she comes into our room.

"Mami, I can't sleep. This bed is too bumpy!"

The bump begins to giggle. Mami lifts a corner of the blanket up. "Marisol! I thought you were lost!"

"I'm going to sleep with Lula." She snuggles close. "Please, Lula."

"Just don't stick your feet in my mouth."

Mami bends down and kisses us both. "Sweet dreams."

"Mami," I ask. "Is Tata sick?"

"He's weak, Luz. He just needs to rest." She turns the light off and walks out of the room, taking her flowery smell with her.

I'm glad Marisol's sleeping with me. Her toasty little body snuggled against me feels like Pepito's. I pull the blanket down, away from her face. "Marisol, you're going to smother under—" She's asleep!

I close my eyes and lie very still. I hear Leon's footsteps and my eyes fly open. He never once came into our bedroom in Chicago.

"Is the coquí keeping you awake, Luz?" he asks softly.

"What's a coquí?"

"A tree frog no bigger than your thumbnail. It sings only at night."

"All I hear is a bird."

"That's a coquí. It gets its name from its song. Listen."

"Koh-keeeeeeee, koh-keeee," sings the little frog.

"The only frogs I've ever heard go 'Glump, glump, glump.'"

Leon smiles. I don't think I ever made him smile before. "The coquí may be able to live in another country, Luz, but it will sing only in Puerto Rico."

"Really?"

He nods.

"Luz, I'm borrowing a car from my cousin, Alberto, to drive to see your grandfather tomorrow. Your mother can't do a thing until she sees him."

"I can't either!"

Leon pulls the blanket carefully over Marisol's bare feet. "We're leaving early. Better get to sleep."

I don't fall asleep. How can I? I woke up in Chicago and go to bed in Puerto Rico. I hunt around in my duffel for my purple glow-in-the-dark notebook. If I wake up with something to write, I just grab for the purple glow.

I told Teresa that the letters I'd write to her would be my diary and that she should keep them for me. She hates to write, so I'll be lucky if I get one letter a year.

Sometime in September 1975

Dear Teresa,

We're homeless! The people who were going to rent us their house decided not to move after all.

We'll stay at my aunt's until we find somewhere to live.

We're going to see my grandfather tomorrow. I'm glad, but I'm a little afraid that he'll look much older. He's had a bad heart attack since I saw him last.

Everything in P.R. is different. Calzados is a dinky little place with dinky little stores. It doesn't even have a library! I should have left my clothes home and taken a duffel full of new paperbacks. Rome said he didn't know we were coming to Dinky-land.

Marisol moves and her arm lands on my chest. I put the notebook and pen under my pillow and take her hand. It's warm.

The coquí is singing. It's where it wants to be. Lucky little frog.

I Meet Felipe

A heavy weight drops on my belly. "Marisol!" I yell. "Get off!"

"Mami told me to wake you up. We have to get ready to go to Tata's."

She starts putting on the clothes she's pulled out of her duffel—black-and-white-striped pants and a green shirt with little red apples all over it.

"Marisol. That combination is gross!"

"I like it!"

"Tata will take one look at you and get another heart attack."

"He will not!" Her lower lip begins to tremble.

I rummage in her duffel and yank out a red T-shirt and hold it next to the black-and-white-striped pants. "Tata will love you in this. I think red is his favorite color."

"You have to wear red too."

"We're twins," Marisol says to Mami as we walk into the kitchen, both wearing red T-shirts.

Mami doesn't even look at us. She's busy packing food in a basket to take to Tata. She must have baked a cake in the middle of the night.

"I squeezed orange juice for you. You have to eat something before we go."

I gulp down a glass of juice and grab a piece of buttered cinnamon toast.

"Here's napkins," Mami says, "and don't get Alberto's car full of crumbs."

The car is sleek and black with tan leather upholstery. Mami, Marisol, and I fit comfortably in the backseat.

"Why does Rome get to sit in the front seat?" Marisol demands, spraying me with toast crumbs.

I pat Rome on the head. "Because he's so cheerful."

Rome turns and makes a grab for my cinnamon toast, but I'm too quick for him.

Compared to the jolting taxi, Alberto's car rides as smoothly as a sled on ice. As we leave Dinkyland, the sky darkens and rain begins to hit the roof and dance off the windshield. Thunder and then a bolt of lightning streaks across the sky. Marisol grabs on to Mami. Rome turns on the car radio, flipping the dial until he gets a band playing rock. His head begins to move to the beat of the music.

"The music's a little loud, Rome," Leon says. "I can't concentrate."

Rome turns the radio off. He slumps back into the seat.

"I only meant you to lower it, Rome, not turn it off."

Rome doesn't move.

With nothing to look at but the backs of Leon's and Rome's heads, I close my eyes. My mind is a racetrack with thoughts speeding around it. What if we can't find a nice house and have to move into an awful one? Far from Tía Ana. With bugs crawling around in the bathtub. I see myself storming out of the house, yelling, "I will not live here!"

I must have said it out loud, because Mami asks, "You will not live where, Luz?"

"In a house with bugs crawling around in the bathtub."

Mami has no patience for my silliness. She looks tired.

Leon drives slowly. The road is bad. Marisol is asking, "When will we be there?" every five minutes. Mami puts her arm around her and hums a lullaby. Marisol's eyelids begin to droop. The next minute she's asleep.

"Rome," I say. "Why don't you put on the radio. Just not so loud."

He doesn't move. I might as well be talking to a wall.

The rain dies out as fast as it began. White flowers are scattered like confetti in the open fields. We pass a farm with horses grazing under an umbrella of trees. Just as Leon says we should be there any minute, we see Tata's big white stucco house. I recognize it from photographs. It looks a little like a two-layered wedding cake. And there's Tata sitting on the veranda. Leon stops the car, and I'm the first one out.

"Tata!"

Tata waves and leans on a cane as he walks toward us. A pain as sharp and fast as that lightning bolt shoots through me. He's not standing straight and tall anymore. I run to him and he hugs me, pulling me against him with his free arm. I reach up and kiss him.

"*Corazoncito!* How good it is to see you."

Mami, Marisol, and Rome surround him. A big turkey bobs up the steps of the veranda, and Marisol giggles and grabs Tata's leg.

Mami is laughing and crying. "Papi. It's so good to see you."

"Conci." Tata's eyes drink her in. He greets Leon with a handshake. We make so much noise with our hellos that we scare off the big turkey. Two more scurry up the veranda steps. Marisol is frightened, so Tata takes her hand and walks up to the big birds.

"Marisol, these are the women of the house, Maria and Flor. The shy one who ran away is Julia. They just want to look you over."

But Marisol doesn't want to be looked over. She runs and dives into a hammock hanging at the other end of the veranda.

"Papi." Mami puts her arm around Tata's shoulder. "When I said you needed a woman in the house, I wasn't talking about a turkey!"

There hasn't been a woman living in the house since Nana Socorro died. A farmer, Ramón, had been leasing some farmland from Tata, and when Nana died, he and his son, Julio, moved into the house to cook for him and take care of the farm. Julio and Ramón aren't here now, Tata tells us, because they had driven to town to get a new part for the tractor.

Tata looks at Mami lovingly. "Constancia, marriage to Leon agrees with you."

Mami smiles. "Leon agrees with me."

"And you, Leon, Constancia has managed to put some meat on your bones."

Leon laughs and pats his belly. "There is much more of me now than when Conci married me."

"See, Papi. I told you I got a bargain."

"Rome, your mother's apple pies have gone straight to your shoulders. I would not like to be your opponent in a football game."

"I take after you, Tata. Look." Rome holds out his hands, showing the moons on his fingernails.

"Moons, yes, Rome, but muscles . . . Ah! The years have turned mine to bananas." He puts out his hands to grip Rome's.

Rome groans and pulls his hands away. "Tata! You nearly killed me!"

"And Marisol and Luz. You are even prettier than my goat."

"That's a real compliment," Mami says. "Now, Tata, no more about goats and turkeys. Let's sit down. We want to talk about you."

"Yes, well, the most important thing about me is that you are all here, healthy and bright. The rest"—he waves his hand—"poof . . . nothing."

It's as if he signaled the rain to start again. The turkeys run cackling to the turkey pen, and Marisol's grown brave enough to chase them.

"Marisol!" Mami calls, but Marisol ignores her and starts to dance and sing, "Rain, rain, go away."

I run down the veranda stairs and grab her hands. "And come back another day!"

"Leave them, Conci," Leon says. "They won't melt."

As I'm twirling around like a five-year-old, we bump smack into a tall boy in a yellow slicker who seems to have dropped from the sky.

"Oh, sorry!" I'm embarrassed and dizzy.

"I shouldn't have gotten in your way."

"What's your name?" Marisol looks up at him, her wet round cheeks bright as apples.

"Felipe. What's yours?"

"Mine's Marisol. And she's Luz."

I try to smile, but it's hard with rain dripping down my nose. "Hi."

"Felipe," Tata calls.

"*Compai,*" Felipe calls back, "I came to see if the rain washed you away, but I see you have company."

"Look, Felipe," Marisol says. "I can do a handstand in the rain." Marisol anchors her hands on the ground and kicks up her legs. She teeters, then topples. Felipe and I try not to laugh.

"Luz is the one who can do handstands," she says breathlessly. "She can do cartwheels too. Will you help me do a handstand, Felipe?" She takes his hand as if she's known him all her life.

I run to the veranda and wrap myself in the big towel Mami hands me.

"Poor Felipe," I say. "Marisol has captured him."

"No, *Corazoncito,*" Tata says. "Felipe is alone too much for a fourteen-year-old boy. This is a treat for him."

"Why is he so alone?" Mami asks.

"It's a long story."

"That never bothers you."

"It's a sad story. I'm too happy now to tell it."

Cartwheels over, Marisol runs to the veranda holding tightly on to Felipe's hand. Mami wraps a towel around her. "Mari-duck, your feathers are soaking wet."

Felipe pulls off the hood of his slicker. His hair is dark brown and curly with rain beads shining in it. His eyes surprise me. They're grass green. Mami invites him to have lunch with us.

"Thank you, but I'm cleaning stables today." He lays his hand on Tata's shoulder. "I wanted to be sure you're okay."

"I'm better than okay, Felipe. Family is a wonderful medicine."

Did a shadow cross Felipe's face when Tata said that?

Felipe leaves and we go into Tata's house to eat lunch. Even though the day is gray, it seems sunny out because the dining room ceiling is bright blue. The heavy wooden table is so large that many more could fit around it than just us.

Mami is disappointed when Tata eats very little of the special dishes she has prepared for him.

"It's siesta and I must rest," Tata says.

As Leon helps him out of his chair, his cane falls to the floor. I pick it up and hand it to him, but he waves it away.

"Leon and I will stroll to my bedroom." Tata takes the arm that Leon holds out to him, and the two walk slowly. Leon says something and Tata nods. They seem to like each other.

Rome takes off to check out the tractor, and Marisol and I beg Mami to let us visit Tata's horse Belleza, but she insists that we strip so that she can throw our clothes in the dryer. We sit wrapped in towels on a purple velvet couch in Nana Socorro's pretty sewing room. Windows look out on a garden of snow white flowers. No other color. Mami opens a cabinet to show us shelves lined with spools of thread with names like russet, mauve, fuchsia, periwinkle. Three large drawers are filled with bolts of fabric, patterned and plain.

Mami lifts out a silky bolt of pale rose. "Oh, how Nana would have loved to make dresses for the two of you!"

I see tears beginning to well up in her eyes, so I say

the first thing I can think of. "Mami, can we look at the fabric?"

"Just fold it when you're done and put it back neatly."

When we're alone I pick material for a dress for Marisol to wear to a ball. Her drenched ponytails are like two leaky faucets that drip water on the blue, gauzy stuff I drape on her. I decide that's not a good game.

Marisol stretches out on the couch, resting her uninvited feet on my lap. "Luz, I like Felipe. Do you?"

"How do I know? I didn't even talk to him."

"You could have if you wanted to."

"How do you know what I could do?"

"Tell me a story about Princess Porcupine. Pretty please, Lula."

If I tell a long enough story, maybe she'll fall asleep. I start. . . . "Princess Porcupine woke up on her pink satin bed. . . ." I do such a good job, I almost put myself to sleep too.

There are voices in the living room. Mami and Leon are talking very softly. I try to hear what they're saying but can't. I wait for five minutes, then, still wrapped in the towel, walk down the hall and into the living room. The voices stop, just as Tata comes into the room.

"Luz, Leon and I need a few minutes to talk to Tata," Mami says. "Did Marisol fall asleep?"

31

"Yes, but when do I get my clothes?"

"Soon."

That can mean anything from five minutes to five hours! I go back to the sewing room and sit down next to the curled-up Marisol. I'm worried. What is it that the three in the living room don't want me to know?

I'm Rude and Beastly and Don't Care One Bit

"I want a pink house." Marisol pouts as Leon opens the front door of a dark blue house that he and Mami rented yesterday.

The muddy blue color isn't the worst thing. The rooms are small and there aren't enough of them. Rome will have to sleep in the living room, which won't make him any nicer to be with.

"When we put the furniture in, it'll look much better," Mami says, smiling. She has a whole collection of smiles. This one is the "pretend everything is great when it's really pretty awful" smile.

This street isn't half as nice as the street Tía Ana lives on. All the houses look like concrete boxes painted different colors, some of them faded or peeling, except for a light yellow one with a blue door and bougainvillea draped over the doorway.

"That pretty yellow house looks as if it's dressed up for a party that the other houses weren't invited to," I say.

"Come," Mami says. This time her smile is real. We follow her through the back door and are surprised to see a backyard that has a bed of tiny pink roses and a tall bush with something black and shiny hanging from one of its branches. An eggplant! A little clay coquí is sitting under a very tall bush with—yes—an eggplant!

"Can I pick it?" Marisol asks, her hand already on it.

"Yes," Mami says, "but when I serve it for dinner, you have to eat it."

Marisol's hand shoots back so quickly that we all laugh.

There's also a banana tree.

"It's very young and healthy." Leon lays his hand on the trunk the way Mami lays her hand on my forehead to see if I have a temperature. "It can grow as tall as an oak and produce as many as two hundred bananas."

"I decided to eat one bite of eggplant," Marisol announces. She pulls on the stem, catching the eggplant as it falls.

"Good catch, but you'd better let me carry it," Rome says, taking it from her.

Mami surveys the yard. "There may even be room for a picnic table." I can tell she's imagining all of us sitting at a picnic table on a perfect summer day, enjoying a good meal.

"Just move the banana tree and you'll have plenty of room," Rome says.

Mami and Leon ignore him. I try but have a hard time because I think he's really funny.

"First we have to buy a kitchen table." Leon suggests that we go into town to pick out furniture in Champas's store. He's sure Luis Champas will give us a fair price.

It's a short walk to the stores. Marisol complains that her feet hurt and she's hungry, so Leon and Rome take turns carrying her on their shoulders. Rome puts her down when we reach the town square. People are selling food: plaintain, roasted pork on a stick, cones of flavored ice, coconuts, and mangoes. Mami buys a carton of brown, flaky things from an old lady with no teeth.

"Take one," she says, holding the carton out to Marisol.

Marisol crinkles her nose. "What are they?"

Leon takes two. "Fried pigs' ears."

"Yuck!" Marisol squeals.

"Taste one," Mami says. "They're like potato chips."

"I don't eat ears!" Marisol's nose is so crinkled, it almost disappears.

I shake my head. "No thanks!"

Marisol points to two kids walking out of the Sun Café eating double-dip ice cream cones.

"Just one scoop," Mami says.

We go into the café and all choose mango nut, even Mami, who's a chocolate freak. Sitting at one of the two white tables in front of the café, we enjoy the ice cream as we watch people go by.

At the furniture store Marisol is really obnoxious. She races up and down the aisles, yelping, "I like this" and "Yuck! Ugly."

Mr. Champas has an oily smile, as if he took it out of a sardine can. When he tells us how much a chair or a table costs, it's as if he's doing us a favor by giving us a cheap price.

We can't get a TV yet. Just beds and dressers, a long sofa bed for Rome that will be our couch, a kitchen table and chairs. One tall lamp, one short. Marisol and

I get one large dresser with flowers painted on the knobs.

The furniture is delivered the next morning. Mami is excited, directing Leon and Rome where to put everything. I pick three pink roses in the backyard. Mami kisses me when I put them in a blue bottle in the center of our new table.

"Luz, you'll begin to like it in Puerto Rico, you'll see. You'll go to school and make friends, and pretty soon it will seem as if you've lived here all your life."

I say nothing, just rearrange the flowers in the bottle.

Leon talks and smiles much more in Puerto Rico. Sometimes his Spanish comes pouring out so fast, I have trouble understanding him. We're supposed to be speaking Spanish because it's a weekday. The compromise Rome fought for was to speak Spanish weekdays and English on weekends. Leon said it would be good for him to speak English or he'd forget everything his English teacher taught him.

"You dare!" Mami had said, smiling.

It's a weekday, and I slip and say something in English.

"Luz, we're in Puerto Rico now," Mami reminds me. "We speak Spanish during the week."

"I know we're in Puerto Rico. Don't think I don't know!"

Mami gets that worried expression as if her skin were on a drawstring and you pulled it tight. But instead of shutting up, I keep on saying things that upset her.

"I'm going to flunk school. I won't be able to understand anything!"

"*You're* going to flunk!" Rome sputters. "I won't make it past the first day!"

"Rome, you'll do better than you think," Mami says. "You have a very good ear."

"I want a good ear too," Marisol says.

"You have one." Rome wobbles Marisol's left ear back and forth. "Needs a tune-up though."

Since we left Chicago, Marisol's the only one able to make Rome smile and act more like himself.

I give her a quick hug, thinking how lucky we are to have her.

There's a knock at the door. Leon hurries to open it. A pear-shaped man in a bright purple shirt and a skinny woman in an orange flowered dress explode into the room.

"Alberto! Sylvie!" Leon slaps the man on the back, then hugs and kisses Sylvie. "Conci." Leon puts his arm around Mami. "These are my cousins, Alberto and Sylvie." To us he says, "This is Tío Alberto and Tía Sylvie. And this is Rome, Luz, and Marisol."

Sylvie is very thin with bony elbows and black hair that almost swallows her face. Alberto is the opposite. His belly folds over his belt like too much dough in a mixing bowl. He smiles under a bushy mustache and pinches Marisol's cheek. "They grow pretty little girls in Chicago." He turns to me. "And very pretty big girls too." He slaps Rome on his shoulder. "Also big, handsome guys."

We pretty and handsome children stand there, looking as alive as fossils.

Alberto and Leon sit on the couch and immediately begin talking business. Alberto's the manager of a big fruit market in San Juan and has promised to sell some of Leon's fruit when Leon gets his farm going. He also agrees to sell Leon's orchids if sales go well.

Mami and Sylvie sit at the kitchen table and talk as if they have been friends for a long time. Tía Sylvie used to teach third grade. Marisol climbs into Mami's lap as if she were a baby kangaroo hurrying into its mother's pocket.

Tía Sylvie moves over, leaving half her chair empty. "Luz, sit here, close to me."

She has a different smell than Mami, a too-sweet smell, like vanilla.

"Your mama tells me that you're afraid to go to school."

I nod yes.

"Two years ago I changed schools. I was so nervous the first day at the new school that I left the bread in the toaster too long and it caught on fire. I threw a pitcher of water on it. That was the end of my toaster."

Mami laughs. "I better not make Luz toast for breakfast tomorrow!"

I shoot off the chair. "Tomorrow!"

"You've already missed two days. The sooner you start the better, Luz."

"I have made arrangements with Señora Rosario, the secretary in the principal's office," Tía Sylvie says. "She'll be glad to walk to school with you tomorrow."

"But I'm not ready to go to school yet!"

"She'll stop by at eight to pick you up. You won't keep her waiting, will you?"

"I might."

"Luz!"

"It's all right, Constancia," Tía Sylvie says. "Luz is just scared, that's all."

"Scared and stubborn." Mami's face is shut against me.

"I have to go to the bathroom." I've learned that being polite helps you get what you want, so I add, "Excuse me, please."

I close myself off in the small room, sit on the toilet lid, and stare at the pink sea horses on the shower curtain. At home I always had a good book hidden away in the sink cabinet for emergencies like this. This sink doesn't have a cabinet, so I'll have to figure something else out.

Being with Tía Sylvie is like having the radio turned on too loud and you can't make it lower. I sneak quietly into the bedroom I share with Marisol. It's square and white. To keep it from looking like the inside of an empty refrigerator, Leon helped me hang three framed photographs that I had had on my wall at home (home is still Chicago): Pepito sleeping on Rome's knee, my eleventh birthday party, and a photograph I took of Mami at the beach. Marisol had Leon put up her poster of baby seals. We almost have to glue our beds together to fit them in the room with our dresser, Rome's dresser, and the dollhouse. Our one window looks out on what is the best thing about Muddy Blue (the name I've given our house)—the wonderful banana tree. I decide to try to finish my letter to Teresa.

Hi again. I'm back. The day after somewhere in September.

You know what they eat here? Fried pigs' ears! I made up a verse about them.

Have you tried
Pigs' ears fried?
I did and died.

There are two of me now. I'm here in P.R., but all the time I think of what I would be doing at home in Chicago.

How was the Wise Girls meeting? Did Shanti come? Or did she really quit the club? Have they cast the parts for the school musical yet? Are you trying out?

I'm having a hard time with forgiveness. I can't forgive Mami and Leon for moving us from our Chicago home and bringing us to P.R. They're happy and expect us to be happy too. Mami seems a little angry that we're not. She's disappointed, I guess.

I start school tomorrow. Everyone will have already been there for two days.

If you don't get another letter, just figure I died on the way to school.

Love,
L.L.*
*Lonesome Luz

School Is Bad, Really Bad

I think the rooster I hear is in my dream. But the ceiling close to my face and the banana tree outside my window tell me I'm in my bed in P.R. Marisol is sleeping, curled up at the foot of her bed.

I pad barefoot into the kitchen, purposely looking droopy. Mami is putting fresh flowers into the blue bottle.

"Mami, I don't feel good."

Mami puts her hand on my forehead, but I back away. "It's my stomach."

"You're hungry, Luz. You've been eating like a bird."

"There's no bread."

"There's time to buy some at the bakery if you hurry."

"I might faint in the street and hit my head against a rock."

Mami holds my chin in her hand so that I'm forced to look straight at her. "Luz, the first day is the hardest. But there's no way to skip it, is there?"

I slump back to my room, dress, get money from Mami, and sleepwalk to the bakery.

In Chicago I used to buy bread from a special bread shop on Fullerton Avenue, where the "el" train rumbled high up along the track, creaking to a noisy stop. People in bright clothes pouring out of the doors looked like a flood of jelly beans. A minute later you'd hear rock music as a guy drove by with his radio playing full blast, his head bobbing to the beat. Boys on skateboards would be practicing flips and jumps, moms would be pushing strollers, boys and girls would walk with arms around each other's waists, sometimes stumbling but never letting go. The public library is near the el station, so most of the time I would bring home a loaf of bread and ten books. I liked the librarian. One day I gave her the bread to check out.

Even though we're on the main street in Calzados, there's nothing to see. I pass the El Toro Rojo liquor store with a mean-looking red bull painted on its sign, and a dressmaking shop, its window displaying a wedding dress that looks like a decorated lampshade. Some scrabbly empty land, and then there's the bakery. Mami said that the owner is Señora Alvarez, who lives in the pretty yellow house with the blue door.

There seem to be only little kids and high school kids living in the houses near us. I would have liked a neighbor to be a girl my age who would turn out to be a best friend. Or just a friend. Two old sisters live in the house right next to us, on the side where the banana tree is. Mami says they're like women left over from a different century. They come out of their house to shop and that's all. Mami will get to know everyone in our neighborhood in a week.

The bread feels warm and I tear off one end to eat as I walk home.

A pair of brown pants hits me as I walk into Muddy Blue.

"I don't care what the rules are," Rome shouts. "I'm not wearing that brown shirt and those pants to school!"

He spots me and throws a blue skirt and blouse into the air. "That's your uniform, Luz! Cool, isn't it?"

Mami had told me that we have to wear uniforms to school, but I had forgotten all about it until Tía Ana had brought them over. I hold up the light-blue cotton shirt and navy pleated skirt.

"You'll look cute in that," Marisol says.

"Adorable," I grumble.

"Change into your school clothes, Luz, and eat breakfast. Señora Rosario will be coming soon."

I really feel sick. Mami's face warns me to get going. I get dressed in my blue clothes and feel like little Goody Two-shoes.

"Good luck," I say to Rome as he and Leon leave, one for school, the other to hop a bus to San Juan to see about a job. Rome's managed to make the brown pants and shirt look like they've been slept in.

Señora Rosario knocks at our door five minutes early. She has squinty eyes and pockmarked skin. Mami says that everyone has something good-looking about them and if you grow to love them, they'll get more beautiful every day. That's Mami. I'll never be as nice a person as she is.

One of Señora Rosario's legs is shorter than the other, so she kind of dips as she walks. She doesn't try to get me to talk. I'm glad about that. It takes us a while to pass all the houses. Other kids are walking to school, and I feel them staring at me. Some have eyes on the back of their heads. Twin sisters walk out of one of the houses and skip by holding hands. A boy as tall as Rome catches up to them. I can hear them laugh. It makes me lonelier than I already am. Finally we come to the school yard and behind it is the school, long with a flat roof. It's in uniform too, the top half painted light blue and the bottom half dark blue. Blue will never be my favorite color again.

"Luz, I'll take you to the principal's office," Señora Rosario says. "Señora Garcia will tell you who your teacher is and what room to go to."

I feel as if someone zipped my chest too tight. I can tell kids are whispering "Look at the gringa!"

Señora Rosario takes my hand, but I pull it away. I can't walk into the school holding her hand! She opens the door and I hurry inside, past all those blue uniforms and the eyes, eyes, eyes.

Señora Garcia stands up from behind her desk to greet us. She is very tall with her hair braided in a crown on her head. She looks like the proud queen in a fairy tale.

"Welcome to our school, Luz."

"Thank you."

"I'll take you to your room. Señor Wilson and your classmates are eager to meet you."

All this can't be happening to me. I'm in a story someone made up. I keep my eye on the black buttons running down the back of Señora Garcia's dress. She opens the door to Classroom 101.

"Señor Wilson," Señora Garcia says to a short, gray-haired man with wire-rimmed glasses behind the desk.

"This is our new student from the mainland, Luz Sorrento."

I'm fifty feet tall, standing there in front of the room. Señora Garcia taps me on the head as she leaves. "I expect to hear very good reports about you."

Señor Wilson asks if I speak Spanish. I say something dumb like "I guess so." He tells me to take the empty seat in the third row.

"Don't worry about doing work today, Luz. Just try to understand what we're doing. If you have a question, raise your hand."

I sit down in the seat, looking straight ahead. Señor Wilson has written a long paragraph on the board. Everyone is copying it. I steal looks at the kids around me. A boy is taking secret bites out of a candy bar. The girl across from me has blond hair. Her head sticks out like a white balloon among black ones. Maybe her mother was Swedish. I'm glad that my father is Italian with black hair and eyes so that I don't stick out as being different. After he left us, I would sometimes look at photographs in one of Mami's albums of all of us together at a picnic or birthday party looking happy. It just made me sad, so I stopped doing it.

English class is next. I follow everyone to the room across the hall. The teacher, Señora Benes, is beautiful. She puts her hand on my shoulder.

"Now, students, what do we say to welcome Luz? Julius, let's hear from you."

Silence. I'm standing there. Now I'm shrinking. I feel my skin being sucked in.

"Julius!" Señora Benes stares at the boy in the first seat of the middle row. He's short and has no neck. His black hair is so messy, he looks as if a wet dog is sitting on his head.

"*Buenas días.*"

"Julius. Speak English!"

Julius stammers, "Welcome to our . . ."

"School, Julius," Señora Benes says in a tired voice. "Repeat after me. School."

"School," Julius mumbles.

I'm assigned a seat in the middle of the room behind a girl with a crooked part and two skinny braids. Her scalp shows pink under her thin hair. Before I've been in my seat five minutes, Señora Benes calls me up to the front of the room.

"Luz, please read the story on page twenty-three aloud." She hands me a blue book. "Now, all of you, listen to Luz very carefully."

The name of the story is "Maria's Happiest Day." I'm numb. I read with no expression. When I finish, Señora Benes asks me to say the word *thirty* for the class. Everyone is supposed to watch and see where I hold my tongue.

My head has drums beating in it. "I don't feel good," I say. "I think I better go home."

I must look as bad as I feel, because Señora Benes walks me to the proud queen's office.

"Just rest on that chair until lunch, Luz," Señora Garcia says kindly. "A good meal will make you feel better."

But lunchtime makes me feel worse. I get in line and take my tray with its plate of rice, bean mush, a too-ripe banana, and a pale cookie. All the hundreds of voices talking, yelling, laughing fill my ears like traffic noise. I'm pushed by kids hurrying to their tables. I can't just stand there! I move to the back of the cafeteria, trying to look like I know where I'm going. I spot a table, empty except for two girls sitting at one end of it. I sit down at the other end and they go on talking and pay no attention to me. I push the food around the plate without eating any of it. I pick up the banana. Is Rome having as awful a time as I am?

I'm halfway through the banana when the girls at the other end of the table squeal and hide their faces.

It's the boy with the wet dog on his head. Julius! He's comes toward me, grinning, with chewed-up banana oozing through the spaces between his teeth. I grab a book and hold it in front of my face. He slaps the book down and grins his banana ooze at me. I put my hands over my eyes until I hear his name called. Probably the lunchroom guard. I open my eyes to see him swaggering over to the guard, who looks furious. She takes his arm and steers him out of the lunchroom.

I throw my half-eaten banana onto my plate of rice and beans. There's no way I'm going to eat it now. Twenty minutes more until lunch period ends. To get through it I pretend to be writing something very important on a pad of paper. "I want to go home, home, home. . . ."

The afternoon in Señor Torres' room passes with me sitting at my desk like a dummy. I know all the words in the spelling lesson, but I keep quiet. I feel a poke, and a boy's voice hisses behind me. "Spell *hospital* on a piece of paper." I tear a small piece off my writing pad and write *hospital* on it. I purposely drop my pad on the floor, and while I pick it up, I push the slip on the desk behind me. "Thanks," hisses the voice.

When the bell rings, I rush out of the room and stand near the front door of the school to wait for Señora Rosario. Julius sees me and shouts so that the whole world can hear, "Hey, Scarface! Where's your Chee-ca-go gun?"

My heart folds up and dies. I'm not alive as I start to walk across the school yard, slowly at first, as if nothing happened, then faster. When I'm almost halfway across,

I start to run. I want to slow down, but I hear footsteps behind me.

"Hey, Scarface!" Something hard jabs me in the back. I stumble and feel myself falling. I hit the ground hard, then lie there, dazed, tasting dust. Stones dig like glass splinters into my knees, elbow, and the side of my face. The footsteps run off in the opposite direction.

I sit up and touch my scar with my fingertips. When I draw them away, I see a streak of blood. I try to pull myself up and feel a hand on my arm. I blink the dust out of my eyes and see a girl peering at me through round black-rimmed glasses.

"Can I help you up?"

I put all my energy into trying to stand. I'm not steady, and Owl Girl tightens her grip on my arm.

"Can you make it to the bench?" she asks.

I nod and we walk slowly, like two old people. I sit down, breathing hard. Owl Girl takes a thermos out of her book bag, fills a plastic cup with water, and holds it to my mouth. I drink.

"Thank you."

"Are you okay?"

"Is my . . . cheek bleeding? Where the scar is?"

She studies the side of my face. "Not a lot. Can I wipe the blood and dust off?"

I nod.

Her face is very close to mine. It seems strange. I don't even know her. She touches my face very lightly with a tissue. "It's not bleeding now," she says. She wets the tissue with water from her thermos and dabs my cheek once more.

The tissue has more dust on it than blood. I take it from her. "Thank you."

We sit there while I rest for another minute. Owl Girl is small with dark-brown wavy hair held back from her forehead with a yellow butterfly barrette, and brown eyes the color of dry autumn leaves. Her mouth is small and perfect and very pink, as if she had been eating raspberries. She closes the thermos and puts it back into her book bag.

"Don't let what Julius said bother you. Nobody listens to him. There's even a rumor that he's going to be switched to a different school."

"I . . . think I better get home."

"I know where you live. I saw your furniture delivered. The house with the banana tree."

I stand up cautiously. My knees burn and feel wobbly. Owl Girl latches on to my arm, and I'm surprised how strong she is. She's very short. We walk slowly.

"Julius—everyone calls him Banana Monster—gave me a hard time when I first started school. I was only seven."

"What did he do?"

"Oh . . . I don't even like to think about it."

When we're close to Muddy Blue, Roberto, the little boy across the street from us, runs into the street chasing a red ball. His mother screams as a brown convertible driven by a bald man wearing dark sunglasses screeches to a stop. She grabs the boy up.

"What do you think you're doing, speeding like a crazy man?" she yells.

"Why don't you watch your kid!" the bald man yells back. He speeds off, leaving a dust trail behind. The little boy, Roberto, is crying as his mother carries him into their house.

"Wow," I say. "It's a good thing that guy's brakes worked."

Another few steps and we're in front of Muddy Blue. "Where do you live?" I ask Owl Girl.

"On Regala, the next street over. In the blue house with the tile roof."

"Oh . . . well, maybe we can walk to school together sometime."

"Maybe," she says, handing me my book bag. And with a small wave she turns and runs as if someone were chasing her.

When Mami Wasn't Home
and I Needed Her

Even before I walk through the door I call loudly for
Mami. She doesn't answer. Leon is the only one in the
kitchen. His face asks me what happened, but when I
squeeze back tears and no words come, he leads me to
my room.

"Is my face okay?" I ask. "The . . . scar isn't opened
up or anything?"

"There's just a small scratch above the scar, Luz.
Nothing to worry about. If you lie down on your bed,
I'll clean the dirt out of your wounds."

"Where's Mami and Marisol?"

"They went for a walk."

Leon returns with a sheet that he spreads out next to me. "Luz, can you move onto this? It will keep your bedspread from getting bloody."

I move as if I'm made of wood. He takes off my dusty shoes and socks and puts them beside my dresser.

"If this hurts too much, tell me."

He washes off the blood that's left on my face with a damp cloth. It hurts and I hold my breath. He looks worried. I never thought he cared enough to worry about me.

"Luz, I have to use a sterilized knife to get the bits of stone out of your knee."

A minute later he's back, and I clamp my teeth together and make two fists when I feel the hot point of the knife. I almost bite my tongue off holding back a howl. The knife digs in again. The howl comes out. "Owwww!"

"That's it," Leon says. "It's over." He shows me three tiny stones. I stare at them.

"They were in very deep." He dabs the hurt spots with disinfectant, and they burst into flame. I bite my lip and taste a drop of blood. Leon brings me a glass of cold water.

"Do you want to tell me how you hurt yourself?"

56

I shake my head.

"Your mother will be home soon. If you need anything, call me."

He walks out of the room and I'm alone. I bury my head in my pillow, careful not to rub my cheek. I would never tell him that a horrible boy called me Scarface. I'll never tell anyone. Ever.

The Many Horrible Deaths of Banana Monster

I had rehearsed what I would say when Mami saw me wearing jeans to school, but when I walk into the kitchen, she looks up from mixing pancake batter and says a cheerful "Good morning." I feel let down. I'm grumpy and aching to be rude to someone.

"I'm not going to wear a skirt to school with my knees all bandaged up," I say fiercely.

"I don't blame you, Luz. But why did you put on your very best jeans?"

I am wearing my oldest, most beat-up pair, and Mami knows it. I ignore her and pour a glass of orange juice. "Ugh," I say. "I hate it when you leave all the gook in it."

"Are you grumpy because your knee hurts you, Luz?"

I drink the juice down, making a face. "No, I'm not grumpy, and yes, my knee hurts. Mostly I'm mad that I fell. Banana Monster must have loved seeing me flat on my face."

"Banana Monster?"

"The obnoxious character who chased me. He runs around the cafeteria with chewed-up banana oozing between his teeth."

Rome walks into the kitchen, and I quickly pop a bite of banana into my mouth and ooze it out between my teeth.

He looks at Mami as if talking to me would be more than he could stand. "I'm going to push a banana into her face."

I slurp the ooze back in. "There are no more bananas," I say sweetly.

Rome grabs a mango off the counter and aims it at me. "It's too good to waste on you. An egg would be better." He opens the refrigerator door just as Mami says the pancakes are hot and ready.

Rome immediately drops the mango in a bowl, and we bring our plates to Mami. "The first pancakes I've made in Puerto Rico." She gives us a short stack and we dig in.

She puts some aside for Marisol and sits down to eat with us.

"I'm going to see the principal today, Luz," Mami says, as she serves us another helping of pancakes. "That boy may hurt someone seriously."

"Mami, don't! Everyone will know my mother went to school."

"How will they know?"

"That kind of stuff gets around."

"She's right," Rome says.

"For heaven's sake, then, Luz, steer clear of him!"

I almost say it's like trying to steer clear of a wild dog, but I stop in time.

"What's the boy's real name?" Mami asks.

"Bozo Blubberbelly the Third."

Mami can't stop her smile.

I'm so generous, I leave the last pancake for Rome.

I'm on a bathroom pass when Owl Girl comes in. We're both glad to see each other. She smiles, showing very straight, white teeth.

"How are all your wounds?" she asks.

"Okay. The good news is that Banana Monster is absent today."

"I had a nightmare about him."

"I did too, but it was funny. I dreamed Banana Monster came to school in his underwear and didn't know it. It drove him nuts because everyone was laughing at him and he couldn't figure out why."

Owl Girl giggled. "I wish I could have that dream."

"Something else is funny. I don't even know your name."

"Rose Carrera. You can call me Rosita. I'm in the other seventh-grade class. What's yours?"

"Luz Sorrento."

"I've never known anyone named Luz."

"I don't think I thanked you enough for helping me yesterday."

"It's okay. You weren't in very good shape."

"Maybe we can walk home together today. We could meet at the flagpole."

"I'd like that."

We say good-bye and walk to our classrooms. English class is okay, but history is so boring that to keep myself from falling asleep I think of horrible ways for Banana Monster to die. My favorite is death by rotting.

He would get some rare tropical disease that would rot away all his bones until nothing was left but a transparent skin like snakes wriggle out of.

When the bell rings, I grab my stuff and go straight to the flagpole. I wait and wait and no Rosita. I'm just about to leave, when I see her puffing along.

"The teacher asked me to water the plants in our room," she says breathlessly.

"I thought you forgot we were going to meet."

"Oh, no!"

We start to walk. "I was so bored in history class, you know what I did?"

"What?"

"I figured out the most horrible deaths I could think of for Banana Monster. You want to hear one?"

"Just don't tell me one that has blood in it."

"This one has a little blood, but it doesn't spurt all over the place. Banana Monster will break out in blotchy, itchy spots all over him, especially in his nose, under his arms, and on the bottoms of his feet, from a rare parasite that winds itself around his heart and slowly sucks all his blood."

"Ugh!" Rosita shivers. "That's awful."

"It serves him right!"

Rosita laughs, and seeing her laugh, I laugh, and each

of us seeing the other one laugh laughs even more, until we don't even know what we're laughing about. We collapse on a bench in a small bit of a park at the far edge of the playground. It has an orange tree, two enormous yuccas, and what once was a cement drinking fountain. We sit in the shade of the tree, and discover the yuccas screen us from view. It's a private little hideaway.

"So what horrible death can you think of for Banana Monster?" I ask, still breathless.

"To burn to death, each part of him catching on fire"—she lowers her voice and speaks each word slowly—"until . . . nothing . . . is . . . left . . . but . . . a . . . toasted . . . skull!"

"Ooooow! . . . You win!"

"Luz, I noticed you have the same purple notebook I have. Which is funny, because I bought mine in San Juan."

"And I bought mine in Chicago. It must mean we're meant to be friends."

Rosita's cheeks turn a little pink. She's shy, I warn myself. Slow down.

"I don't use it as a diary, do you?" she asks.

"I'd be bored writing about what happens in my life every day."

"So . . . what *do* you write about?"

"Oh . . . different things. Poems mostly. They're

really personal, so I hide the notebook in my room. If Rome got a hold of it, I'd die."

"Is Rome your brother?"

I nod. "I have a sister too, but she can't read yet. And then there's my mother and stepfather."

"I wish I had a brother and sister."

"So it's just your mother and—"

"My father died when I was eight," she says quickly, as if wanting to get over that information fast. "My uncle—my father's brother—lives with us part of the time. He was the one who was racing that brown convertible when the little boy's ball rolled into the street."

"Does he always drive like that?"

Rosita flings one hand out as if to get rid of a fly. "He's crazy, Luz. He says he sells used cars, but my mother worries that he's mixed up with drugs, and that he lives with us because no one would think to look for him in a little place like Calzados. I hate him! He's awful to my mother!" She covers her face with her hands, and I hear little squeaky noises that sound as if they're coming from a kitten. I sit there, helpless.

She uncovers her face, sniffles, and wipes her cheek with the back of her hand. I pull a crumpled piece of Kleenex out of my jeans pocket and hand it to her. She blows her nose and starts to hand the tissue back to me.

Then she giggles and stuffs it into her own pocket. "I guess you don't want *that* thing back."

I'm so glad to see her smile that I hug her. She doesn't hug me back. She probably doesn't come from a hugging family like mine. (I don't count Leon.) A wave of love for my kissing, hugging family washes over me.

"You haven't told me what you write in your notebook," I say.

"Mostly fantasies. About little people—elves and gnomes and fairies."

"Your stories must have magic in them, then."

Rosita nods. "Lots."

"I wish there were magic in real life." I reach over the back of the bench, pick up a fallen tree branch, and wave it in the air. "Ab-ra-ca-dab-ra. Make the Muddy Blue change to a big white house with a porch and an attic and flowers all around."

I hand the branch to Rosita. She whips it around so fast, I have to duck. "Make my crazy uncle burn up so we can use his toasted skull for a garbage can."

"Poor crazy uncle!"

She waves the branch more slowly. "Make my father alive again."

She hands the branch back to me. Her wish has made her sad. I say nothing. I'm learning not to fill every silence with talking.

"My father knew he was going to die," she says so softly that I move closer to hear her. "He had cancer." I wait, still saying nothing. "While he was still strong enough he recorded twenty stories on tape so he can tell me a story every night like he did when he was alive. My mother comes in bed with me and we listen together."

"It's wonderful that he did that."

"I like it best when I fall asleep while he's talking so I don't hear the recorder shut off. Then I feel he's really been with me."

Her eyes look dreamy.

"Rome has two cassettes of my father playing the saxophone. He's played them for me once. He can't play them when Mami's around."

Her eyes ask what she's too polite to put in words.

"My father . . . left us," I say. "My mother never talks about him."

Rosita puts her hand on my arm. "I'm sorry."

I shrug. "It's old stuff."

"I get a saxophone mixed up with a trumpet."

"They both can sound very moody or happy or romantic. . . . I guess my father was really good."

She stands and picks up her book bag. "I better get home. My mother won't know where I am."

We start walking. "Maybe you can come over to my house sometime," I say.

"I . . . don't go to other kids' houses."

I look at her, surprised. "Never?"

She shakes her head. Her expression stops me from asking why.

"But I can meet you at the corner of Regala and we can walk to school together."

"Sure. Eight-fifteen?"

She nods and we say good-bye. I watch her walk down Regala until she stops at a light blue house with a palm tree that looks dead. She turns and waves. Then she slips through the door of her house like a letter pushed into a mailbox slot.

So many questions run around in my mind that they fall over each other. Why doesn't Rosita go to other kids' houses? Is her crazy uncle a drug dealer? Why is he awful to her mother?

And I've seen her only twice. How much more is there?

After dinner Marisol falls asleep with her clothes on. Mami and I carefully tug them off and fit her legs and arms into her pajamas. Her head flops on her pillow like a rag doll's, but she doesn't waken. Mami bends and kisses her cheek and sits down on my bed. I stretch out and rest my head in her lap.

"I walked partway home with that girl I told you about. Her name is Rose but she's called Rosita."

"I hope you get to be good friends, Luz."

"She's small. But she's got a big mind, if you know what I mean."

"What *do* you mean?"

"Well, I think terrible things happening to you makes your mind bigger because you do a lot of wondering."

"What terrible things have happened to Rosita?"

"A lot. Her father died when she was eight from cancer. And then she has this awful uncle living at her house. Her mother thinks he might be a drug dealer."

Mami nods. "That certainly is a lot for a thirteen-year-old to handle." She strokes my hair. "And what's going on in *your* big mind, Luz?"

"Nothing much," I say, but Mami doesn't believe me. I'm thinking that having a father who leaves and forgets you may be harder than having a father who loves you and dies. "It's . . . too hard to talk about, Mami."

"It's often the hard things that need talking about the most."

I press my face against her softness. "I can't, Mami."

We sit like that for a while. Quiet. And then I ask Mami if she misses all her book group friends.

"We've been away so short a time, Luz. But I know I will. Very much."

"I don't think there's a book group in Calzados, do you?"

Mami kisses the top of my head. "You never know."

She checks Marisol's cover, throws me a kiss, and walks out of the room. When I crawl into bed I listen for the coquí but I don't hear its song. I miss it. I miss a lot of things. I try to fall asleep so I won't remember what they are.

Can Dogs Bark
in Spanish?

"Lula," Marisol cries. She runs toward me, her ponytails bobbing, her little shoes pounding. I'm moving pretty fast too. It's Monday of my fourth week of school, and I'm always eager to get home.

"Pepito's coming tomorrow!"

"Marisol, are you sure?"

She dances up and down. "Mami just got a letter from Tía Luisa. She says Pepito's too lonesome without us. He won't eat."

I rush into the house and grab Mami's hand as she's standing at the sink. "Is Pepito really coming?"

"Yes!"

"What?" Rome comes into the kitchen and drops his book bag on the floor. "Pepito's coming?"

"But we have to figure out how to pick him up at the airport. Leon is going to see about a job. And I promised Mrs. Vargas that I'd watch Roberto while she goes to the dentist."

"I'll pick him up," Rome says. "I'll take a *público* to the airport."

"I'll go with Rome, Mami. He'll need help."

"You'll both miss school."

"School won't miss me," Rome says. "Let Luz come. She'll help me with Pepito."

Mami looks at me anxiously. "The airport is such a big place. . . ."

"Mami," I beg. "Please!"

"No big deal," Rome says. "I'll hang on to Luz."

Mami sighs. "Just use the brains God gave you, Rome."

October and still no letter from you!

Hi Teresa,

Wonderful, marvelous, terrific news!

71

Pepito is too lonesome without us so he's coming to Puerto Rico tomorrow! I'm going with Rome to pick him up at the airport. He'll have to learn to bark in Spanish!

October 3, but you'd never know it. 80 degrees! No pumpkins anywhere. Just bananas, bananas, bananas!

More later.

I jump out of bed at six o'clock. Rome is awake too. At breakfast Mami tells him at least twenty times to hang on to me.

"Conci, Rome and Luz are just going to the San Juan airport, not to Africa," Leon says. He gives Rome the claim ticket for Pepito that Tía Luisa sent, and Rome puts it in the wallet he got for his birthday. Leon gives him some extra money. Just in case.

It's been a long time since I've done anything special with Rome. I don't mind that he doesn't talk much. It's nice just walking together with both of us so excited about getting Pepito.

There's a *público* parked in front of the *farmacia* with two people in it besides the driver. They have cameras around their necks and wear matching flowered shirts, so it's pretty clear they're tourists. If I were a tourist, I'd carry a camera in a book bag and wear black.

I feel a spurt of excitement as the driver starts the motor.

The airport's jammed. People are rushing in different directions. I grab Rome's arm, certain that if I lose track of him, I'll never find him again. A man pushing an old lady in a wheelchair is coming straight at me, and when I jump away, I bump into a mother carrying a crying baby.

"Sorry," I say. The baby yells louder.

I pull on Rome's arm. "Do you know where you're going?"

Rome doesn't answer.

"Rome!"

"Just follow me!"

Whenever Rome isn't sure of what he's doing, he gets grumpy.

We walk a little farther, and then we see the information booth. Rome talks to a cheerful information lady, who tells us we have to go to the baggage claim downstairs.

The news is bad. Pepito's flight has been delayed an hour.

"Rome," I groan. "What'll we do for an hour!"

"Wait," Rome says. "Let's go back upstairs."

We take the escalator upstairs and sit on an empty

bench. I look at the huge metal clock suspended from the ceiling. Its hands are as big as shovels. Five minutes seem like five hours.

Rome takes a folded sheet of stationery out of his pocket and looks at me, embarrassed. "Luz, I wrote this letter to Cindy. I want you to correct any spelling mistakes, but . . . can you do that without reading it?"

I laugh. "That would be pretty hard."

Rome fingers the letter. "Don't say anything about what I wrote. Okay? Just correct it."

"Okay."

He gives me the letter with a pencil to make corrections.

While I read, he wanders around. He has written the letter carefully, with green ink, to match the cute little coquí sitting in a bottom corner of the stationery. I see how much work he has put into the letter. I would hate it to have a lot of mistakes.

The first thing he tells Cindy about is the coquí. I put an accent mark over the last syllable of *coquí*. So far so good. Then he tells her about visiting Tata. He misspells *engine* and *rhythm*. One of his sentences is so long that I chop it in half to make two sentences. He tells Cindy how much he misses playing football. Hockey's dead for sure. No ice except in refrigerators.

Boring weather. He never thought he'd get tired of sunshine. He hopes she thinks of him sometimes. He thinks of her all the time. Could she please write him a letter? He signs it "Love, Rome." The word *love* seems smaller than the others. As if he were bashful to write it.

Rome is at my side the minute I lift my head. "Were there a lot of goofs?"

"Just a few. They weren't bad though." I would like to tell him that it was a very nice letter. But I don't dare. I hand it to him.

"Thanks. So it wasn't bad, then?"

"No."

He pockets the letter carefully.

I can't help saying, "It's good."

He looks relieved. "Thanks."

He sits down, his legs stuck out in front of him.

The shovel hands are moving so slowly. I close my eyes.

"Luz!" I feel my hand being pulled. "Let's go."

I shake myself awake and run down the escalator with Rome to where suitcases are rolling onto a moving sidewalk. Everyone crowds around, looking, looking, then grabbing their duffel, suitcase, package, as it rolls by. Pepito can't come rolling down that sidewalk!

"There he is!" Rome shouts. He runs toward an

attendant carrying a traveling cage. Pepito's brown eyes are peering through the grate in the cage door.

Rome thrusts the claim ticket at the attendant. "That's our dog!"

Pepito begins barking like mad. Rome is so excited, he fumbles with the cage door and finally gets it open. Pepito runs out and I scoop him up, hug him, and kiss his cold little nose, but he wriggles loose, jumps to the floor, and starts running in circles and barking.

"He's all mixed up, Rome. He doesn't know where he is."

Rome picks Pepito up, holds him against his chest, and talks to him gently. "Pepito, it's okay. You're going to be with us now. See, it's Luz and Rome." He strokes Pepito's silky head. Pepito stops wriggling and I put my hand out to him. I can see the exact second when he recognizes me. He licks my hand, and when I take him from Rome, he licks my cheek.

"He knows us now, Rome."

Rome scratches him under his chin. "I hope he likes P.R. better than I do."

A Very Special Gift

Rosita and I meet at the flagpole every day after school and go to what we call "our" park. If we sit at the end of the bench, the orange tree shades us and we're hidden behind the yucca. We've never seen anyone there except once. Gretta, the blond girl in my class, was sitting on the bench with a boy's arm around her. The two of them flew off like scared pigeons when they heard us coming. Gretta has ignored me ever since and I'm not sure why. It bothers me to have someone look right through me.

"That happens to me a lot," Rosita says. "Kids look right through me as if I were cellophane."

"You're probably just imagining it."

She shrugs. "I don't imagine bad things. I don't have to. There are so many. I just imagine good things."

"You mean more bad things, besides your father dying and your crazy uncle?"

"Oh, you know, orphans, people getting beaten up, starving dogs with their bones sticking out . . . cancer . . . war."

"What are the good things you imagine?"

"The first one is that my mother can see again. She's blind."

"Oh . . ." I swallow hard.

"I don't go to other kids' houses because I don't like to leave her alone too long."

"I could come to your house."

She hesitates. "I'd be afraid my uncle might come home."

Questions run around in my mind, but I don't ask any of them. We're both quiet. Then Rosita begins to talk.

"My mother was fine until she was twenty years old. But then she got the eye disease that her mother had." She turns away and talks to the ground. "I worry I'll go blind too."

"Oh, Rosita! Just because—"

"I have nightmares that I wake up one night and open my eyes, but everything is black. So I think my eyes are still closed and I try to open them again, but I can't because they're open already."

"Oh, Rosita . . ." I fling my arms around her. She begins to shake like Pepito when he's scared. I feel the wetness of her tears on my cheek.

She pulls away, takes off her glasses, and wipes her face with the back of her hand. Her naked eyes are so sad that I long to comfort her, but I know that whatever I say has been said to her a hundred times.

"My mother was already blind when I was born."

"So . . . she's never seen you."

"She's a sculptor, so every year on my birthday she sculpts my face just from what her fingers tell her I look like."

"So . . . there are thirteen sculptures of you?"

"No! My uncle knocked the two-year-old one down when he was in one of his fits."

I wince. I see Rosita's face falling to the floor, breaking into bits.

"The sculptures are my mother's photograph album. Me at two years old is gone now. Even my uncle felt bad. He tried to glue the pieces together, but there were too many of them."

A lump clogs my throat as I think of the three fat albums Mami has filled with photos of Rome, Marisol, and me.

"Enough of this serious stuff." Rosita reaches around my back and takes hold of my hair. "Can I braid your hair, Luz? I just learned how to make a French braid."

I say okay, but I never wear a braid. With my hair pulled back my scar shows up too much.

"I braid my mother's hair. It comes down to her waist." When she finishes braiding my hair, she unpins the butterfly barrette from her hair and clips it to my braid.

"I'm giving you this barrette, Luz. It looks pretty in your hair."

"Rosita! I'm not going to take it. You wear it all the time."

"I want you to have it." She straightens the barrette and stands back to look at her handiwork. "Perfect."

"Well . . . if you ever want it back, just ask me."

"Luz, you're so serious. What are you thinking about?"

"Oh, just my own stuff."

"Luz . . . I wish you would tell me."

"Well . . . when you said your mother is blind . . . I got such a sinking feeling. Part of me was sad. And part of me felt . . . really ashamed that I've made such a big deal about a scar on my face."

"My mother would understand that the scar is a big thing for you."

"And then . . . all I'm worried about is myself, and you're worrying about orphans, sick people, hungry dogs with their bones sticking out. . . ."

"You didn't have the father I did, or you'd worry about them too."

"What do you mean?"

"My father's job was worrying about people. So I learned it from him. He was a social worker." She pulled me off the bench. "You're too serious!"

"Serious. Me?" I take her hands and spin her around the way I spin Marisol. She doesn't feel much heavier. We laugh and collapse on the scraggly grass. We lie there, catching our breath and looking up at the sky. Rosita checks her watch. It has a silver band and looks more like a woman's watch than a kid's. Her mother would have no use for it now.

"I'd better get home," she says.

We pick up our book bags and start to walk.

"I'd really like to meet your mother, Rosita."

"She'd like to meet you too."

At the corner of Regala we stop. "Maybe I will some-day."

"Someday," she repeats, but not as if she means it.

I don't walk into Muddy Blue right away. I go to the backyard and sit against the banana tree. It's uncomfortable, but I don't move. I think of Mrs. Carrera's blindness and of Rosita having those terrible nightmares. No one in our family wears glasses. Not even Tata. We're so lucky and we don't even know it.

Whoever Thought I'd Miss My Lime-Green Toothbrush?

November 20. *And still no letter from you.*

Dear Teresa,

Pepito reminds me of me. He runs around and can't settle down. It would have been good if Tía Luisa had sent his old rug so that he'd have something familiar to curl up on. Just like I want to keep my old lime-green toothbrush. It reminds me of washing my teeth in our bathroom in Chicago. I put the new red one Mami bought in my underwear drawer.

Leon tries to be cheerful, but you can see it's phony. He's gone to look for a job while he waits for news about the land, but no one wants to hire him. He's come back to P.R. because it's his home, and he's treated like he's from an alien planet. I don't get it. Mami is so bored that she's trying to find a job teaching English. No luck so far.

School is a little better. The English class is the best because the teacher is letting me be pretty much on my own. Mostly, I write about Chicago. I used to get jelly knees when my teacher asked me to read my story out loud. But I'm used to it now and the kids seem pretty interested. The one who really likes them is a girl, Gretta, who I had some trouble with at first. She started ignoring me because I had seen her in a park with a boy's arm around her. Silly, I know. But I kept saying hello to her anyhow and then helped her with an English lesson so we're okay together now. I eat lunch with her and her friend, which is better than eating alone. The best thing that's happened is that I met a girl, Rosita, who is different from anyone I've ever known. We've become very good friends and see each other every day. I wish I could eat lunch with her, but she eats at a different time.

I can't believe it's November. It rains sometimes, but most of the time it's warm and sunny. I remember the first day it's warm in Chicago, everyone celebrates, dumping coats and hats, having picnics, roller-skating. I don't miss those cold, blah November days in Chicago. The coldest it ever got in Puerto Rico was 39 degrees! And that was for one day.

Rome has made a shoe-shining box and goes into San Juan on Saturdays with a friend, Carlos, to try to make a little money. He doesn't spend it. He's saving for something, but he won't tell me what.

Today is Saturday and my cousin Juanita and I are going to spend the day together. I've been with her once and I like her a lot. She teaches botany at the University of Puerto Rico, so one thing we're going to do is go to the university Botanical Garden. She told me that more than 200 different kinds of palm trees grow there. (I'm polite enough not to tell her what I think of palm trees.) She and Leon talked about orchids as if they were talking about their babies.

Pepito is on my bed now. He's circling around, trying to find a place for himself. Poor little gringo dog.

Writing a letter isn't so hard, Teresa. Sit down with a pen and a piece of blank paper and write on the top, Dear Luz. Begin with what you ate for breakfast if it gets you started. Then keep going.

This is the longest letter I've ever written. Be sure to keep it for me!

> Your friend with the lime-green toothbrush,
> Luz

I lean back in the seat of Juanita's small bright-red car. It's nice to get a holiday from everyone, even Mami. I think worrying can be catching. I'll feel perfectly okay about something, but Mami worries about it so much, I begin to worry too.

Juanita has very straight, very short jet-black hair and dark brown eyes with perfect arched eyebrows. Her nose is a little too big and her mouth is a little too small, but put it all together and she's glamorous.

"Luz, guess what?" she says, smiling. "I'm *not* going to ask how you're doing in school and if you made any friends yet."

I look at her gratefully. "Thanks."

"Is there anything that you'd like to do after we see the Botanical Garden?"

"Tío Alberto told me about a famous fort in Old San Juan."

"El Morro. You can get great views of the ocean from one of the watchtowers. El Morro's in Old San Juan, so after we look around we can eat in a little café that I like. Then if there's still time we can go and look at the harbor. I have to start back at four. I have a dinner date with my friend Michael."

"Sounds great," I say, and wonder about Michael. Tía Ana is really worried that Juanita isn't very interested in marrying.

The garden is one of the most beautiful places I've ever seen. Green everywhere—cool, feathery ferns, pillowy moss that I want to lay my cheek against, a tree with white blossoms hanging like bells from every branch. We walk along a forest of ferns and see sparkling water plunging over rocks. We stop for a while to look at orchids with colors so deep—gold, orange, wine red, pale green, purple—you feel your eyes drinking them in.

"Juanita, Leon would love these orchids!"

"Remember to tell him about them."

We move along and I point to an orange flower with a deep purple ruffle. "That flower's so beautiful, I can't believe it's real!"

"Luz, the most beautiful things *are* the ones that are real."

I think about this. Juanita asks, "What is more beautiful than a fiery sunset? Or a hummingbird?"

"So why do people always say, 'That's so beautiful, it doesn't look real.' Why did *I* say that?"

"You were repeating, not thinking. We all do it."

We've reached the lotus ponds. White and light purple flowers rest on large heart-shaped leaves that lie flat on the water.

"Those lotus leaves look like water beds for fairies," I say.

Juanita laughs. "Do you like to write, Luz? I would think you do. You have quite an imagination."

"Yes. Stories in school. But for myself I write poems."

"I'd love to read one sometime."

"Well . . . I don't show my poems to anyone. Not yet."

"I'll just wait until you do, then. Will you put me on your waiting list?"

I smile at the thought.

You couldn't go to a place more different from the Botanical Garden than El Morro. The fort is huge, old, and dead.

Juanita tells me that the Spanish built El Morro over four hundred years ago to protect the island from enemies. "They did a good job. An enemy has never been able to take over the fort in over four centuries. The British almost did, but they were beaten by dysentery."

With Juanita hanging on to my leg, I climb up and walk on the fortress wall as if it were a wide sidewalk. When I look down, I decide to get back to the stone floor very fast. El Morro is on a point of land that sticks out into San Juan Bay. The heaving water below me doesn't look very friendly.

"The walls are twenty feet thick," Juanita says. "Even the great U.S. Navy couldn't penetrate El Morro. But as you know, the United States defeated Spain anyhow, and they were given Puerto Rico as part of the peace treaty."

"I don't know anything about Puerto Rican history," I confess. "We never learned any of that in school."

"How did you think Puerto Rico became part of the United States?"

I am feeling more stupid by the minute. I shrug. "I guess I never thought about it."

"It's not your fault. The way Americans teach history you'd think Puerto Rico fell off the map."

When we stand in one of the domed lookout towers, I gaze down the shoreline at a long strip of one- and two-story shacks that seem as if they're piled one on top of the other.

"That's La Perla," Juanita says. "In Puerto Rico even the slums have an ocean view."

We agree it's time to eat and drive to a little café called the Smiling Coquí. It's a cheerful place with bright blue walls and ceiling, Puerto Rican travel posters decorating the walls, and flowers on every table.

Looking at a poster of El Morro, I say, "Rome might like to see the fort. No point in asking him though. He's decided to be Mr. Miserable."

We sit down and Juanita moves the flowers to the side so we're looking at each other instead of at a lily.

"It's hard to make such a drastic move at his age, Luz. I'm sorry he's taking it so hard." Juanita folds her arms and leans forward on the table. "And tell me about you."

The waitress comes at the perfect moment. I can pay attention to the menu instead of to Juanita's question.

"They have great *sancocho*, Luz."

When I learn that's vegetable stew, I pass on it and order *pasteles*. We both choose mango flan for dessert.

Two men wearing baseball hats are sitting nearby. One of them is talking fast and his face is almost as red as the salsa dripping from his taco. He slams his fist on the table, making his cup of coffee rattle.

"I bet those men are arguing about whether Puerto Rico should be independent or not," Juanita says. "Their faces are so close together that they could eat each other's tacos." She smiles. "Puerto Ricans tend to be very emotional."

"I'm emotional! I know that!"

"So you qualify to live in Puerto Rico."

"Do you think Puerto Rico should be independent, Juanita?"

"When I was a university student and very young and passionate, I did. Now I have doubts."

"What does Tata think?"

"Don't ask him that when we're trying to have a peaceful dinner!"

"I know, Juanita. Tata's old and passionate."

Juanita laughs. "Luz, it's easy to see why Tata loves you so much."

We're eating our flan, when Juanita asks if I'm hoping that she's forgotten her question about how I'm doing in Puerto Rico. When I answer yes, she says, "Well, I have. For now."

She pays the sleepy cashier and we leave the car where it is and walk around for a while.

I like Old San Juan better than new San Juan. It's small, just about seven blocks in each direction. We walk along a street paved with bluish bricks. The stucco houses are two stories high and are painted quiet colors. My favorite is a yellow house with tall arched windows and a balcony dripping with pink and red bougainvillea. I imagine a handsome young man in a red satin suit playing a guitar and singing to the beautiful señorita on the balcony above.

"Old San Juan is kind of romantic," I say.

"Our first evening out together, Michael and I had dinner in a very romantic restaurant about a block away from here."

"With candlelight and soft music?"

"How did you know?"

"Oh . . . movies and books. Did you have a cupid fountain with water rippling into a pool?"

"Hey, can I borrow some of your books?"

"I wish I had taken them! There's no library in Calzados."

"I'll have to drive you to the San Juan library sometime so you can stock up."

The ride to the harbor takes longer than it should have because of the Saturday traffic. Lucky again, we find a parking spot in the shade of a tree. The breeze blowing off the water feels wonderful. I hold my face up to catch it as if it were rain. We ignore the souvenir stands and walk along a pier where the giant cruise ship *La Isabella II* and four smaller ones are docked. The water is blue-green, but around the ships it looks smudged and oily.

"More than seven hundred cruise ships dock here a year," Juanita says. "They're like floating cities with swimming pools, restaurants, game rooms, libraries."

We have fun imagining ourselves on the deck of *La Isabella II* as it cuts through the blue water. We're relaxing in our sequined bikinis on the sundeck, each of us reading a good book and drinking a tall frosted drink.

The pier is crowded and we dodge two little kids who run to the edge of the pier and scare their parents half to death. Juanita shields her eyes with her hand. We both forgot sunglasses. Marisol probably hid mine.

"Luz . . . is that Rome?"

"Rome! Where?"

"Ahead of us, near the juice stand."

My eyes follow her pointing finger. I catch sight of Rome's salmon-colored shirt, but then it's gone.

"Rome!" I yell. I run to the juice stand, but I see no one. Was he a mirage? The rest rooms are right there, so I go in. How can you make yourself pee fast? I finish and push through the bathroom door, practically bumping into Rome as he walks out of the men's room.

"Rome!"

He's not glad to see me. His hair is long and ratty-looking. When he's feeling low, he stops taking care of himself.

"What are you doing here, Luz?"

"What are *you* doing here? I thought you were shoe-shining."

"No customers, so I just took off."

"How did you get here?"

Before Rome can answer, Juanita runs up to us. "Luz, you took off so fast! Rome, how nice to see you."

"Hi," Rome says. No smile.

"Doing some exploring?"

"Yeah, a little."

Rome is acting like he's half dead. I want to shake him.

"I have to leave for my date with Michael, Luz. Rome, would you like a ride home?"

"Yeah, thanks."

Still no smile.

When we find the car, Rome climbs into the backseat.

"Nice car," he says.

"It drives like a dream," Juanita says.

I lean back against the seat and try to think about the Botanical Garden and the Smiling Coquí and our walk on the blue-brick streets. When we finally get to our house, I hate to say good-bye to Juanita.

She climbs out of the car to hug me. She even hugs Rome, which must feel like hugging a sack of flour. Then she blows us a kiss and drives faster than she should down our street.

"Luz." Rome's eyes drill into me. "Forget you saw me at the pier, okay?"

I stare at him.

"Okay?" he repeats.

"Why?"

"Just forget it. I'm counting on you."

He goes into the house and I follow. Mami and Marisol are baking cookies. Marisol's licking the mixing spoon.

"Luz, how was your day?" Mami asks.

"I had a great time with Juanita. I'll tell you about it later. I'm beat."

Marisol holds out the spoon. "Want a lick, Lula?"

There's not a drop of frosting left, but I lick the spoon anyway. "Thanks, Marisol."

I collapse on my bed and stare at the ceiling. A conversation I had with Rome bobs up in my mind like a cork that's been underwater. We were walking Pepito and he told me that his shoe-shine friend's brother had stowed away on a cruise ship going to New York and he just called to say he was fine. The trip hadn't cost him a dime. A couple of sailors had hidden him in their room.

I remember how excited he had seemed.

I feel cold. As if a wind off the ocean had penetrated the room.

A Promise

It's November and it's hot! I just can't get used to the weird weather. Even the nights haven't cooled off. Everyone seems to be crabby. Leon finally got a job driving the Champas's furniture delivery truck, and he's exhausted when he comes home at night from trying to steer that monster truck through the crazy Puerto Rican traffic. The pay is low. Leon says he has no bargaining power to ask for more. Rome is really miserable, because it's the beginning of the hockey season at his old school.

Even Mami is grumpy. Tonight there were so many dishes and pots that it took us forever to clean up. She's not even out of her apron before Marisol pulls her to the couch to read a book. She insists that Mami read her *Pokey Little Puppy,* which Mami has read two nights in a row. When Mami said she's tired of that book, Marisol starts to sob.

I can see Mami is about to lose it, so I pull Marisol into our room. "I'll read it," I say. As I settle her in my bed, I hear Mami.

"Leon, I need to get my head into something other than the laundry basket. . . . I haven't seen a movie since we got here. We can't even rent a video. And I can't even make a telephone call to my sister."

Leon's voice is much softer. I can't hear what he's saying. But the next day a man from the telephone company installs a phone in our house. Mami begins to make telephone calls to schools to find an opening for an English teacher.

"What will you do with Marisol if you go to work?" I ask.

"If I can get part-time work, Roberto's mother may take care of her. I'll figure something out."

It's a beautiful night with a silver moon in a sky the color of violets. Rome drags an old beach towel out to the yard so he can sleep outside. I ask Mami if I can sleep out too. "I don't think so, Luz . . . I don't know if it's safe."

"She'll be okay," Leon says. "*Nothing* happens in Calzados. Not even robberies or muggings."

"I'll take Pepito," I say. "He barks like mad when he hears a footstep a mile away."

Marisol starts jumping up and down, begging to be able to sleep with us.

I make my fingers crawl up her arm. "It's a real buggy night with lots of slimy lizards crawling around."

"Yuck!" Marisol squeals.

That gets rid of her fast!

Rome stretches out near the patch of roses. Pepito looks at him and then at me. Rome doesn't say anything, so I walk as far away from him as I can, smooth away stones and sticks, and lie down on an old sheet close to the banana tree. Pepito settles next to me, his head resting on my stomach. Rome's voice comes floating through the night.

"Why are you way over there? I'm not contagious."

I pick up my towel and settle myself nearer him, but not too near. Rome always needs space. His face against the sky looks like one of those black paper cutouts. He's perfectly still. Pepito lies down between us and I reach over and coax him to come closer to me. I like to pet his silky fur.

Quiet. One minute. Two minutes . . .

"Rome, if you're going to lie there like a stone, what did you call me over for?"

Quiet. I let out a long, breathy sigh.

He turns his head toward me. "I hate when you sigh like you're a hundred years old."

"That's how old I feel sometimes."

"Why? It's not so bad for you here."

"How do you know?"

"Because you don't make an ass of yourself in school every day!"

"And you don't have an obnoxious monster yelling Scarface at you!"

This hurts him. I knew it would.

He grabs my braided hair. "You look pretty good in a braid."

Anything to change the subject. "Thanks," I say grudgingly.

"Luz . . . I guess I embarrassed you when we were with Juanita."

"I just don't want her to think I have a nerd for a brother."

"That's what living in Puerto Nerdo has done to me. Turned me into a nerd."

Rome has started calling Puerto Rico "Puerto Nerdo." Mami doesn't like it. Leon doesn't seem to care. Little things don't bother him, which is good. Rome has been pretty awful to him since we left Chicago. Not that that's a little thing.

Last night, waiting for Leon to come home for dinner, Mami told us something we didn't know. I was cutting tomatoes for a salad, Rome was setting the table, and Marisol was stringing wooden beads. I'm sure Mami told us the story so that Rome would know about some of the pain in Leon's life and how good a man he is. She wanted Marisol and me to know it too, but mostly Rome.

"Leon has a younger brother, Thomas, not much older than Rome," Mami said. "He was born when his parents were quite old, so Leon was almost like a father to him. Thomas dropped out of high school and got on drugs and Leon used all his savings to send him to a private school, hoping he would do better. He did for a while. But . . . he dropped out and disappeared. Leon tried to find him for two years, then gave up. His parents had died by then, so he left Puerto Rico and came to Chicago. It's very sad for him. He won't talk about it."

"So." Rome sits up and scratches in the dirt with a stick. "Last night Mami told us that Leon has a brother. I don't see what difference that makes to us."

"It makes me think there are a lot of things we don't know about Leon."

"I know all I want to know."

"You sure have been doing your best to let him know that you don't like him."

"If not for him, I'd be out on the ice now, playing hockey. I miss it, I miss the guys."

"You were hoping Dad would come back and Mami and he would get together again."

"Weren't you?"

"Yes, but not as much as you."

"I don't believe that."

I pull Pepito onto my chest and talk into his fur. "At least you know Dad loved you."

"What?"

My chest tightened. "He never really loved me."

"What gave you that crazy idea?"

I sit up. Pepito deserts me to lie down next to Rome. "Let's not talk about it, okay?"

"You brought it up."

"I shouldn't have. Forget it."

"I think disappearing the way Leon's brother did is a copout." Rome shifts to his side and looks at me. "If I ever got back to Chicago, I'd at least write."

"Would you want to go back to Chicago even if we didn't?"

"In a minute! I'd live at Tía Luisa's and graduate high school, then take a year off to work until I had enough money to buy an old wreck. I'd fix it up, pick up one of those stray dogs on Fullerton. 'It's just you and me, Buddy,' I'd tell him, and head out on Eighty West. Just me and my dog. Free."

His words chill me. I feel the ache of having him gone and he's still right beside me. "Leon should get that piece of land soon and things will be better."

"I won't be here long enough to find out."

"What's that supposed to mean?"

"I have plans."

"What kind of plans?"

He grabs my braid again and tickles my nose with it. "My plans are private, Nosy."

"Rome, why didn't you want Juanita and me to see you at the pier?"

"Luz, be a pal, will you? You never saw me. Okay?"

Now it's my turn to be a stone.

His eyes catch a glint from the moon. "Luz, promise, please?"

"Okay, okay!" But even as I say that I worry it's a promise that I might not be able to keep.

Sometimes Things Really Do Work Out!

Time is moving faster than it did when we first arrived in Puerto Rico. It's already December. The plans to visit Tata were made very fast when Juanita called and said she would be able to drive us to his farm on Saturday. Tía Ana, Mami, Marisol, Juanita, and I are going. Leon needs Rome's help on the delivery truck.

Juanita and Tía Ana walk into the house Saturday morning, and it's as if a fresh breeze blew in. There hasn't been much laughter or fun going on in Muddy Blue.

"*Muñequita!*" Tía Ana swoops Marisol up. Her kiss leaves a purple lip print on Marisol's cheek. She takes a handkerchief out of her purse to wipe it off, but Marisol runs into the bathroom to look at her cheek in the mirror.

"I like it, Tía Ana," she calls. "Can I have one on the other cheek?"

"One is enough. I have to save the other one for Tata."

Juanita has brought a plant in a pretty bowl that she carefully puts on our new bookcase by the window. "This is especially for Leon," she says. "It's an orchid from the Botanical Garden."

Mami gives Juanita another hug. "Thank you."

It's not easy to fit our stuff *and* us in the car. Marisol ends up sitting on Mami's lap.

"I should have rented a truck!" Juanita says. "You're bringing enough food for a wedding!"

Tía Ana does most of the talking as we drive. You've heard of long distance runners? Well, Tía Ana is a long distance talker. It's a good thing she makes us laugh.

The sky is hanging low, as if it were a blue curtain not tacked up tightly enough. A car speeds around a curve on the narrow road and heads straight for us. Juanita swerves sharply.

"*Ay Dios mío!*" Tía Ana raises her fist at the driver, who is already out of sight. "Men are babies! They like to show off even if it means getting killed!"

Tía Ana has no breath left after that. Marisol falls asleep in Mami's arms. I close my eyes. Tía Ana and Mami think I'm asleep and they start talking about a tumor in Tata's stomach.

I'm instantly awake. "Mami, what's this tumor you're talking about?"

"Luz, Tata is fine. The tumor isn't dangerous. Tata can live with it and it won't hurt him."

"What is a tumor anyway?"

"Remember how your toe swelled when you stubbed it? A tumor is a swelling inside your body."

"It stays in him, then?"

"Yes, it's very slow growing."

"You mean it grows!"

Tía Ana smiles. "It must sound awful, but it really isn't dangerous."

"Is that what you and Leon were talking to Tata about?"

"I see what you mean about Luz having to know everything," Tía Ana says.

"Is it?" I repeat.

Mami nods. "Yes."

Tía Ana has gotten her second wind. I tune her out until I hear the name Michael, but she doesn't say anything interesting except that she hopes Juanita won't shut the door in his face the way she's done to her other boyfriends. When she and Mami start talking about jobs and how hard they are to find, I put myself in a kind of trance and am surprised when Juanita calls, "End of the line."

Before Tata can even get up from his chair, we pile out of the car and surround him. He has to be hugged and kissed by all of us.

Tía Ana and Mami don't think the village woman does a good job keeping Tata's house clean. They lug the vacuum cleaner out and hang the Indian rugs on a clothesline to air. Juanita gives herself the job of pruning some of the bushes.

"I have a surprise," Tata says. I take his arm as we walk down the veranda stairs.

"This way, Tata?" Marisol calls, running ahead of us.

"Yes." We walk to the side of the house, where a stone path leads to the white flower garden.

"Nana collected seeds for every variety of white flower she could find," Tata explains.

"It looks like it snowed," Marisol says.

Tata smiles. "Puerto Rican snow."

Marisol climbs onto a bench at the edge of the garden that has a design of white roses worked into the blue tile.

"I made that bench for Nana when my fingers worked better than they do now." Leaning on his cane, Tata bends slowly to pull out a prickly weed. "Felipe must have missed that one. He keeps the garden weeded."

"Tata, is this white garden the surprise?" Marisol asks.

"No. The surprise I'm thinking of moves."

Marisol giggles.

"Come." We go through the garden and off into some trees, where Tata opens a gate to the animal pen. "There are two surprises. See if you can find them."

We walk into the pen and look around. The turkeys are pecking at feed. Flor sees Tata. Gobbling loudly, she runs to greet him.

Then I see the surprise! Two baby goats are snuggled close to their mother, Estrellita. "Marisol, look!" Marisol squeals and starts to run. I grab her hand. "We don't want to scare them, Marisol."

Marisol is so excited, she jumps up and down.

"They're just a week and a half old," Tata says.

The babies are gray and white. They both have pink noses and little stubs for horns. I take Marisol's hand and walk very slowly until we're close enough to see their lemon-yellow eyes with the black slit pupil. Estrellita turns her head. Her eyes are the same lemon and black. I have to tell Juanita that I've added a goat's lemon-yellow eyes to our list of beautiful things.

Marisol tiptoes up to the babies. "Tata, they look exactly alike!"

"They're twin girls."

Estrellita gets to her feet, walks over to Tata, and presses her face against his leg. The twins skitter after her. The white-faced one starts chewing Marisol's shoelace.

"Hey!" Marisol shrieks, and yanks her shoe away.

Startled, the twins begin running around in circles, then leap onto a boulder, jump down, and start butting each other. They're so light on their feet! They jump straight into the air and come down on the same spot.

"Tata, what are their names?"

"You and Marisol are going to name them."

"I'm going to name the white one Lily," Marisol says. "Like the flower."

"Why don't we think about it a little, Marisol," I say.

Before we leave the pen, I pet Estrellita on her forehead, and she presses against me. "I didn't know goats were so friendly, Tata."

"If you give them love, they give it back."

Belleza is in a pasture on the other side of the house, and it takes a while to walk there. Tata moves very slowly. We come to a small blue stucco house almost hidden by tall hibiscus bushes.

"Is this a surprise too?" Marisol asks.

"I built that cottage for my oldest sister, Angelina," Tata says. "She died last year. I like to think she is still living in it, watching the hummingbirds drink out of the red hibiscus."

"Can I look inside?" I ask.

Tata nods.

I open the blue door and find myself in the prettiest room I've ever seen. The furniture is light wood with light blue cushions. The white wallpaper is decorated with hummingbirds sucking nectar from blue morning-glories. A painting of a pond of water lilies hangs on the wall over a small desk crowded with letters and books. The room works its magic on Marisol too. She stands next to me and doesn't run in and start touching everything.

"Has anyone else lived in it?" I ask.

"No. The right person hasn't come along yet."

"Tata, if I could live in this blue house someday, I could become a great poet."

I'm joking, but Tata nods solemnly. I hug him. "Tata, I love you."

Marisol and I walk into the sunny bedroom. Tata tells us he has it cleaned once a month. I lie down on the quilt-covered bed.

"I feel a poem coming on," I say, dramatically pressing my hand to my forehead.

"Lula is being silly, Tata."

The kitchen is small and neat and has a white table that would seat only two people. A perfect house for two small people . . . Rosita and her mother?

"Good-bye, house," Marisol says as we close the door behind us. Tata trips over a jagged stone. I reach out just in time to help him get his balance.

"Once I held your hand and helped you walk. Now you help me, isn't it so, *Corazoncito mío*?"

Marisol runs ahead to where Belleza is drinking water from a trough.

"Luz!" she yells. "Look. Belleza has a scar just like you."

Marisol is pointing to one of Belleza's back legs marked with a long, dark line in her beautiful white hide.

"See, Luz. See the scar!"

I don't answer.

"Belleza grew frightened in a thunderstorm," Tata explains. "She tripped and fell against some barbed wire."

"Luz fell too!"

"Marisol, shut up!" I pick up a handful of hay, and Marisol screeches and runs behind Tata.

Tata takes out sugar cubes from his pocket and

hands one to me. "Give it to Belleza, Luz. She'll get to know you. You want to learn to ride her, don't you?"

I say yes, and hold out the sugar cube on the flat of my hand. Belleza's mouth feels wet and rubbery as she swishes the sugar off.

Tata gives Marisol a sugar cube, but when Belleza swings her big white muzzle close to her hand, she drops the sugar. Belleza eats it off the ground.

I do want to learn to ride Belleza, but now that I'm standing next to her I feel scared. When you stand close to a horse, you realize how big they really are.

"Time for lunch," Juanita calls as she runs to catch up to us. She puts her arm around Tata's shoulders. "Ana made your favorite *asopao*."

Tata sighs. "Eat. Eat. Ana's always trying to stuff me."

Tata is right. *Eat* is Tía Ana's favorite word. If she were a tree frog, she would sit on a branch and sing, "Eat, eat."

Mami has set the table on the veranda, and it looks summery with bright yellow picnic dishes and yellow napkins. Juanita arranges some of Nana's white roses in a glass bowl and sets it in the middle of the table.

"Now Nana has joined us," Tata says, smiling his thanks.

Tía Ana looks like a well-fed parrot with her purple

dress half covered with an orange and yellow apron. She breathes heavily as she carries a black pot brimming with her thick *asopao*. She ignores the white tureen that Mami has set on the table and begins ladling soup into our bowls.

"Soup tastes better from the pot," she announces, glancing at Mami. Tía Ana loves a good argument, and Mami frustrates her by not giving her a chance to have one. She hovers over us, ready to pounce and refill our bowl as soon as we've hit bottom. I have to whisk my empty bowl out of her reach.

We're on dessert, eating pineapple cake, when Felipe walks by.

"Felipe," Tata calls.

Felipe waves and walks up the veranda steps. My heart is suddenly set on fast forward.

Tía Ana practically pushes Felipe into a chair and sets a huge piece of cake in front of him. When Tía Ana gives up trying to get us to eat any more, Tata tells Felipe to forget weeding the garden today.

"Take Marisol and Luz to get some coconuts, Felipe. They will enjoy that."

I feel shy with Felipe at first. But he doesn't act stupid or macho like a lot of boys. Before I know it, I'm having a good time.

A very good time!

P.S. I'm Not Saying a Thing

Felipe greets Belleza by rubbing his nose on her smooth muzzle. "Belleza," he says, "I want you to meet Luz and Marisol." He looks at Marisol. "Do you want to pet her?"

Marisol vigorously shakes her head. Felipe laughs.

Belleza stands quietly as he puts a harness across her back equipped with baskets at each side.

"One minute." He runs to the stable and comes back with a long pole. "Bamboo. To knock the coconuts down if I can't shimmy up to pick them."

A warm drizzle begins to fall. Felipe doesn't seem to care, and we start off for the coconut grove. In the distance we can see the trees against the smoky gray sky. By the time we reach the grove we're soaked.

"The trees are big umbrellas," Marisol says, standing under the thick thatch of leaves.

"I like to climb the trees to get the coconuts," Felipe says, "but the rain makes it hard." He lifts the bamboo pole. "Better get out of the way!" He strikes the pole against a big, hairy coconut, but it holds fast.

"Not ripe enough," he says.

He surveys the tree and strikes another coconut five or six times. It loosens and falls, hitting the ground with a dull thud. Marisol runs to pick it up, but it's too heavy for her.

Felipe picks it up and puts it into one of the baskets. Belleza is eating a tuft of grass and doesn't seem to notice. He hands the pole to me. "Your turn."

I look up into the umbrella of green leaves and try to see which coconut I should attack. They all look the same. As I raise the pole it waves back and forth. I grip it more tightly and give a coconut a hard whack. Nothing. I whack again. No one is more surprised than I am when it falls.

"Good job," Felipe says.

He knocks down two more coconuts, then takes a small machete out of a leather holder strapped to his waist. "Which one do you want to drink from, Marisol?" he asks. Marisol points to the biggest and with a strong stroke Felipe slices the top off one of the coconuts.

"Take a drink," he says, and holds the coconut to Marisol's mouth and tips it.

"Yum." She wipes a dribble off her chin with the sleeve of her T-shirt. "It's sweet!"

Felipe hands the coconut to me and I drink the cool, clear supersweet liquid.

Felipe takes a long drink. "You can finish it," he says to Marisol. He walks deep into the grove of trees and comes back with a big boat-shaped leaf. "My sled," he says.

He leads us to a steep grassy hill, Belleza following. Marisol and I watch as he runs to the top of the hill, the "sled" balanced on his head. He sits in the middle of the leaf, which he tells us is not a leaf at all but a *yagua,* the hard shell that covers the leaf. He pushes at the ground to get the *yagua* moving. It gathers momentum on the wet, slippery grass, going faster and faster. He shouts, hanging on. I start running down the hill but lose sight of him as the sled curves around a bend. Then a splash as the *yagua* hits water. Marisol and I run until we see Felipe knee-deep in a small pond. He's laughing. Drops of water glisten on his face and his white T-shirt sticks to his skin. He leaps out of the pond holding the *yagua* above his head.

"Want to try it?" he asks me.

"Sure." Marisol is at my heels as I run to the top of the hill. I set the *yagua* on the grass and settle myself in the middle of it. It doesn't feel much like a sled.

Without warning Marisol pushes me, sending me careening down the slick grass before I'm ready. I catch at the grass and manage to slow the *yagua* down enough so when I round the curve I don't pitch headfirst into the water but slide off the *yagua* and into the pond on my bottom. I lie for a minute like a beached whale. I'm laughing too hard to get up.

"I want to do it!" Marisol cries.

Felipe takes her hand and starts running up the hill. I lose sight of them. When I hear Marisol screech, I climb out of the water to see what's going on. With Marisol sitting between Felipe's legs, the two of them are sailing down the hill, Marisol screaming with excitement. As they head for the water, Felipe grabs Marisol, leans to one side, and tumbles them onto the grass. Marisol scrambles up and runs into the pond. I follow and catch her slippery little body before her head goes under. Her face is one big wet giggle.

The drizzle has stopped and we climb back up the hill and lie down in the grass to dry.

After a while Felipe says, "Well, I guess it's time we start back." He stands up and stretches. His T-shirt is still damp and he pulls it off and sticks it in a basket with the coconuts. The sight of his smooth chest and muscled arms make me look away. My blood tingles the way it did when I jumped into the cool pond water.

"Do we have to?" Marisol looks at Felipe, but he resists her pleading eyes. We follow Belleza as she walks, the baskets sagging with the weight of the coconuts. My shorts and thin T-shirt are sticking to my body. I congratulate myself for wearing a brassiere.

Dear Teresa,

I'm at Tata's now. I'm staying overnight because Julio and Ramón, who live with him, are in San Juan until tomorrow morning. Mami and Tía Ana don't think he should be alone.

I went sledding today! No, it didn't snow. A rain-wet, grassy hill can be very slippery. The sled is the brown shell that covers a palm leaf before it opens. Felipe, who lives close to Tata, showed me how. He's 14. He's easy to be with because he's so unhung up. His father will be driving me home Sunday afternoon.

Rosita and I see each other every day. We're both reading the same book so we can talk about it.

Two girls from my school live on my street but they're in eighth grade and don't bother saying hello. Most of the kids on our street are still in diapers. There's one little boy, Roberto, that Marisol likes to boss around. He's 4.

I have an idea. Write a letter to me for Christmas. It'll be a present. And I'll write you an extra long one.

Love from Luz

P.S. I know what you're thinking. That I have a crush on Felipe.

P.P.S. I'm not saying a thing!

The Tiny Crack

I like being alone with Tata. Especially at night. We're sitting on the veranda, and it's very quiet now that everybody's gone.

I ask Tata if I can say good night to the goats and Belleza and he says yes. In Chicago I had to be in the house before dark, as if something awful might happen if I weren't. I hated that. But here away from the city, night is a safe friend.

I don't need a flashlight. The moon is so bright that it's easy to see the baby goats snuggled against Estrellita.

I kneel down and look into their little sleeping faces don't touch them. Estrellita is wide awake, watching me. "I won't hurt your babies," I say. I rub her forehead. "Pleasant dreams," I say. As I walk out of the pen I can feel her cool lemon eyes on my back.

I decide not to visit Belleza because it would keep me away from Tata too long. He asks me if Marisol and I have thought of names for the twin goats yet.

"Marisol wants to name one Lily and the other Billy. But I don't. It's too . . . cutesy. Anyhow, it would confuse them."

"Do you know why goats have such short tails, Luz?"

In anticipation of a story, I climb into the heavy rope hammock that tumbles you to the floor if you don't balance yourself right. After being dumped twice, I've become an expert.

Tata leans back and his face gets its "storytelling look." His hands, resting so quietly on his lap, remind me of two sleeping doves.

"Long ago and far away lived a lion who was very proud of being King of the Forest. He lost no chance to tell anyone he met what a great and powerful king he was."

Tata's soothing voice and the gentle swinging of the hammock make me dozy. I fight to keep my eyes from closing. . . .

I startle awake and blink. I'm not quite with it. I realize I did fall asleep.

Tata's dark eyes shine. He smiles. "Sledding uses a lot of energy."

"I can't remember anything about the story you were telling me."

"It's over a hundred years old. It can wait."

"It's just that . . . I felt so safe and cozy. . . . Just like Estrellita's babies."

"Marisol made you angry, Luz, didn't she, when she talked about your having a scar like Belleza?"

I don't answer.

"With or without a scar, Belleza is a beautiful horse. Luz, look at me."

I drag my eyes up to Tata's. They're as clear as rain.

"With or without a scar you are a beautiful girl, *Corazoncito mío*."

He says that because he loves me. I blush anyhow.

"Do you believe me?"

I turn away from his eyes and shake my head no.

"I'm an old man. Old men are reputed to be wise. So you must believe what I tell you."

I look at him again because I know he's smiling. "Maybe you're not old enough, Tata."

"Oh, *Corazoncito mío,* I am very very old." He

reaches for the glass of water on the table beside him. I start to help him but then don't. He doesn't like being helped with ordinary things. His hand shakes and I have to look away. I'm relieved when he puts the glass back on the table.

"Luz, there's a tribe of Pueblo Indians famous for their beautiful pottery. When one of the Indians makes a pot that's perfect, she makes a tiny crack in it to show that it's been made by human hands. Being human means being imperfect, Luz. So . . . your scar is like a tiny crack in a perfect bowl."

"Tata, I have a million cracks!"

"A million?" Tata wags his head at me, then pulls himself up from the chair. I walk with him to his bedroom and take his shoes off and give him his slippers. In the morning I'll polish his shoes.

"Promise you'll call me if you need anything during the night. Okay?" I bend down and kiss his cheek. He kisses the top of my head.

"Good night, *Corazoncito mío.*"

"Tata, can I sleep in the hammock?"

"Be sure you're warm enough. Take a blanket and a net."

"I will."

I put on a long nightshirt; get my notebook, pen, and a light blanket; and walk barefoot to the veranda.

As I lie in the hammock, I think of what Tata said about the tiny crack in the Indians' pots and I am filled with love for him for trying to make me feel beautiful.

I swing back and forth, back and forth, looking up at the stars spilling across the sky. Do I love Tata so much because on top of all the love I feel for him I also give him the love I never had the chance to give my father?

Managing to sit upright in the hammock, I light a candle on a nearby table. I open my notebook and lean closer to the candle flame. Which of the images swimming in my head do I want to capture in a poem? What could be better than the moment I'm living right now? I write a line and scratch it out . . . I pause . . . I forget everything—the baby goats, Felipe, my father, everything—as I sound out words in my brain, choosing, rearranging, searching. I write two lines and lie back in the hammock and then sit up and write some more. I read the lines aloud. The poem stops but doesn't end. It needs a closing line . . . maybe two. I don't have them. I read it again.

Under the bright moon
The breeze rustles the bougainvillea
Lacy moon shadows dance on my legs
Tata rocks in his carved wooden chair
Crik, crik, crik.
The swinging hammock hums

Ko-keeeeee, sing the tiny tree frogs
Brik, brik, brik, chant the crickets.

I close my notebook. I think of the wildflowers I once pressed between its pages. Now I'm pressing words and they are just as fragile.

An Okay Day Turns Terrific

I'm worried. Tata doesn't look good to me. I wonder if he called for some water during the night and I didn't hear him. He's still in his slippers. I take that as a bad sign. Tata always dresses from head to toe the minute he gets out of bed.

"I know how to make coffee, Tata," I say. "I'll bring it to you on the veranda. I make good eggs too."

"No need. I'm not hungry."

I ignore him the way Mami does and scramble two

eggs with lots of goat cheese. Tata says I'm a great cook and eats most of what's on his plate.

After we finish eating, Tata settles himself in his rocking chair to read.

"Tata, I'm going to pull a few weeds in Nana Socorro's garden."

He waves as I run down the veranda steps. Marisol is right. The white garden looks like a small field of snow. As I kneel to pull out a bushy weed growing between two rose bushes, I see a sparkling green bug on one of the leaves. It crawls onto a stick I hold out and then onto my finger. I like the whispery feel of its thread-thin legs walking on my skin. I can see a bright yellow stripe on its belly. I turn my finger to see the stripe better, when I feel someone standing behind me. Felipe.

"I didn't want to scare your bug away," he says.

I try to coax Miss Yellow-Stripe onto Felipe's finger, but she's had enough of us and flies away.

Felipe looks younger somehow, and I decide it's because the red kerchief tied around his head makes his hair stand up like a little kid's. The green T-shirt he's wearing makes his eyes even greener.

"Your grandfather wants me to help you walk Belleza around so you'll get to know her," Felipe says. "Is that okay?"

"Sure," I say, and think, Tata, I love you!

Belleza is glad to see Felipe. He strokes her forehead and she presses her head against him.

"Belleza is my best girlfriend," he says. "Right, Belleza?" He holds out a carrot and in a second she's chomped it down. After he puts a halter on her he gives me the reins. "She'll follow you."

It's like putting a leash on a car and walking alongside it with its motor running.

"Luz, you're putting Belleza to sleep!"

I speed up a little. It's hot out and the perspiration is trickling down my back. Belleza leads me across the pasture until I can see the blue house hidden behind the giant hibiscus.

"Turn her around and go back to the drinking trough," Felipe says.

I turn slowly, hoping Belleza will follow me. She doesn't. I look at Felipe.

"Give her reins a sharp tug. Don't be afraid."

But I am afraid, and Belleza knows it. She stands still, then, totally dismissing me, chomps off a tall tasseled grass stem with one quick movement of her powerful jaws.

"You did pretty well for the first time. We can cool off at the coconut pond if you want. Belleza loves to munch on the wet grasses."

Belleza behaves and follows alongside me. She must

know where she's going, because as soon as we sight the pond, she moves more quickly and sinks her muzzle into the cool greenness.

"We can munch too." Felipe unties a plastic bag from his belt and takes out two *empanadas* wrapped in paper napkins. He hands one to me. We sit down and kick our sandals off. Felipe puts his feet into the water.

The *empanada* is still warm. I take a bite. "Ummm, thank you," I say. "Your mother is a good *empanada* maker."

"My father's the cook in our family. My mother's never around."

"Does she work?"

"She's an interior decorator. She lives in San Juan during the week to be near her clients."

"So she comes home on weekends?" Felipe doesn't answer right away. Maybe I'm being too nosy, but it's too late to take my question back.

"She and my father worked it out so that she would be home Friday, Saturday, Sunday, and Monday morning. It never happens. If she comes home Saturday and Sunday, we're lucky." He shrugs. "I try not to expect her. Then if she comes, I'm surprised."

"Was she home more when you were little?"

Felipe frowns. "I wasn't little for very long." He takes

a bite of *empanada* and chews it slowly. "When she didn't come home for my birthday last month, I felt worse for my father than I did for myself. He had baked my favorite chocolate cake and made a special dinner."

I feel terrible for him. "She probably was really sorry she couldn't be with you," I say.

"Oh, she's always sorry. Then when she does come I'm so angry at her that it's hard to have a good time."

"My grandfather told me your mother gave you a horse for your twelfth birthday."

He pulls his feet out of the water and looks at them as if he's never seen them before. "What would you rather have, a horse or a mother?"

I say nothing. I feel too much.

"My horse, Noche, is beautiful. She's all black with a white blaze on her forehead. You're welcome to come and meet her anytime."

"She and Belleza must look great together."

"Ummm, they do."

We both eat the rest of our *empanadas* without talking. Then Felipe stretches out on the ground, resting his head on his hands. I lie down too.

"If not for my dad, I'd live with my uncle in New York City."

"It would be like going to a different planet."

"I'd like to go to art school there."

"You're good in art, then?"

"I like it better than anything else. That doesn't mean I'm good at it."

"You wouldn't like it that much if you weren't."

"What do you like to do?" He smiles. "Except twirling around in the rain?"

"Write poems. And read."

"I like to read, but I've never tried to write a poem."

I'm so hot I pick some cool grass and hold it against my forehead.

Felipe pulls the kerchief off his hair, wets it in the pond and, saying it will cool me off, ties it around my ankle, then smooths out the ends to look like a bow. "See. I'm artistic. That's the one thing my mother likes about me. She says I take after her." He picks up a stone and pitches it into the pond. "I hate when she says that."

"I don't know what my father says or thinks. I never see him."

"Oh. Leon isn't . . . ?"

"My mother and father are divorced. Leon's my stepfather."

"That's funny. I thought you looked like Leon."

"Me? Look like him?"

"Hey," Felipe says, "it's not an insult. I think he's good-looking."

My face burns up. I'd like to plunge it into the pond.

"So your father never visits you?"

"It bothers Rome much more than it bothers me. He was closer to him than I was."

"How old were you when you last saw him?"

"Almost ten."

"Then you had pretty many years with him."

"Pretty many years . . . ?" I flop over on my stomach and talk to the grass. "He didn't love me, so it was no years at all."

Felipe talks to the sky. "That's exactly the way I feel about my mother."

Belleza has moved so close, I can hear her chomping. I sit up. "Belleza's close enough to give me a haircut," I say. Anything to break free of talking about my father.

"I've been wondering, Luz, why did you come to live in Puerto Rico?"

It's the first time Felipe has said my name. It sounds beautiful. I don't answer right away. I want to hang on to the sound a little longer.

"You don't have to answer," he says.

"Oh, I don't mind. My mother and Leon were born in Puerto Rico, and they decided they wanted to return home. Rome and I didn't want to come. But they never asked us. So, we're here."

"Well, your grandfather's in Puerto Rico, and your aunt and Juanita. And Belleza."

"And the little coquí," I say.

What if he knew that I added *and you* to that list?

Christmas Miracles

Hi Teresa!

Getting a Christmas card from you was a miracle! I would have liked it if you had written more than a five-sentence message, but I read it over and over and that made it seem longer.

Christmas isn't as big a day in Puerto Rico as it is on the Mainland. Puerto Rico is part of the United States, remember? So they call where you live (and I don't anymore) the Mainland. January 6, Three Kings Day, is much more important. Children put out boxes of straw for the Three Kings' camels on the night of January 5, then in the morning the straw is gone and there are presents in the box. Leon made a pretty box for Marisol and since there was no hay around she filled it with pieces of tomato, pineapple, banana, and a peppermint candy. Rome whispered to me that the poor camel that ate the food in Marisol's box would get a bad case of the runs. In the morning she found a bracelet, new hair ribbons, a box of colored paper clips, and one of Leon's favorite chocolate bars. So she did all right.

Even though it seemed weird that Christmas was a sunny day with flowers blooming and lizards skittering around, we didn't want to give up celebrating it. Mami, Rome, and I went to church in San Juan with Juanita and Tía Ana on Christmas Eve. The EC Catholics, right? The service was what we're used to. What I liked best was being out at night in San Juan.

The great thing was that Tata felt well enough for Ramón to drive him to our house, so it was our first Christmas with him. And Rosita and Mrs. Carrera came too! That was really special. It made up for not having a white Christmas.

Instead of buying a plastic Christmas tree (no evergreens here) we strung colored lights on our big eggplant bush. After dinner, when it was dark, we sat out in the yard with the lit-up eggplant bush and had coconut ice cream and pineapple tarts. Rome and I entertained everybody. Instead of singing "O Christmas tree, O Christmas tree," we sang "O eggplant bush, O eggplant bush." This year with so little money for buying gifts we got only books for presents, except for Tata's. He had carved a white horse, Belleza, to put outside our dollhouse. Another Christmas miracle is that Tata can still carve such small, beautiful things. I made everyone a hand-painted card of an eggplant bush strung with Christmas lights. I figured it was an international exclusive, because no one else in the world would be painting a lit-up eggplant bush with the star of Bethlehem shining on it.

It's too hot to wear red wool and fur, so Santa wore a bathing suit and came riding in on a surfboard! See what I mean about things being different in P.R.?

Love, Luz

P.S. I hope you're remembering to save my letters!

The Sardine and the Cricket

Pepito jumps off the couch, where he's not supposed to be, and barks as excitedly as if I had been gone for months instead of a school day. I pick him up.

Leon's sitting at the table, the newspaper open in front of him. "Hello, Luz."

"Hi. Where's Mami?"

He turns to look at me. "She received a call to come in for a job interview. Marisol's at Roberto's house."

"What kind of a job?"

"Her note didn't say."

"You're home early, aren't you?"

Leon sighs wearily. "A truck full of pineapples ran a red light and sideswiped me, denting the rear fender of Champas's truck. He fired me."

"He fired you? That's not fair!"

"Champas isn't bothered with what's fair or not."

"You don't even seem angry."

"If I let my anger out it would be bad for all of us." Leon stands up and stretches as if waking from a deep sleep.

"Champas is such an oily man. Like a sardine." I shudder.

Leon seems even taller than usual. I am sure he has lost weight since coming to Puerto Rico.

Mami and Marisol walk into the house with two breads they had bought at the bakery. Mami smiles at me and then sees Leon. She walks over and kisses him. "Did Champas give you a little holiday?"

"A very long holiday. He fired me."

Mami drops the breads on the table. "He's a fool! What did you do? Jump on one of his Posturepedic mattresses?"

Leon kisses Mami's cheek. "Only you can find something funny in it."

Pepito hears Rome's step and runs to the door. "What's going on?" Rome asks when he sees all of us in the living room.

"Leon got fired," Mami says. "For jumping on one of Champas's Posturepedic mattresses."

For some reason this breaks Rome up. He laughs so hard, we all laugh. Leon tells him about the dented bumper and then asks Mami about her job interview.

"It was with Raul Perez, the owner of the *farmacia* Ana works for. He needs someone who is bilingual and a good typist. He's skinny with heavy-lidded eyes and reminded me of a cricket. He told me that my responsibility would be to run the office. Because I was inexperienced, he would pay me only half of what the salary will eventually be, *if* I satisfy him. Meanwhile he was eyeing me in a way that made me distrust his use of the word *satisfy*. So I wished him good day, bought an ice cream cone, and walked home."

Rome hoots. "That cricket was a wolf!"

"So," Mami says, looking at Leon sympathetically, "this has not been a lucky day. Are you okay?"

"I'm going to work off steam and finish polishing the car."

Leon had bought a beat-up car from a neighbor and had been working on it for two weeks. Yesterday he said to Mami, "Now you can drive to Ana's or anywhere else you want to go." He had ushered her to the car, and Mami climbed in, turned the ignition key, and the engine started right up. He had treated each of us to a candy bar to celebrate.

I decide to help him polish the car bumpers. I don't do too well. The rust is stubborn.

"Just spit on the rag," he says.

I try. "Not enough spit." I can almost see my face in the bumper that Leon's polished.

"How did you get it so shiny, Leon?"

"Spit."

Pepito runs out of the house and jumps at the rag in my hand, catching an end between his teeth. He yanks and I yank. I finally give up.

"Hey, Leon, what about dog spit?"

He laughs and it makes me feel good.

Heavy Stuff

Marisol is pestering Pepito, and he's run under the couch to get away from her. Mami has to finish cooking dinner, and she asks me to read to Marisol. When Leon comes in from his new job in the stockroom of a San Juan supermarket, we wait awhile for Rome to get home. Mami keeps looking out the window.

"Luz, you're sure you have no idea where Rome might be this late?" Leon asks.

"No, but he's not really *that* late."

"Try telling your mother that."

Leon takes a quick shower while I set the table, and Marisol unsets it. She collects the plain blue napkins and insists on using paper napkins that say "Happy Birthday."

"I guess it's *somebody's* birthday today," I say grudgingly.

I don't know if Mami is angry at Rome or just worried. Probably both. Our dinner is getting all dried up, so we begin eating without him.

No one talks as Mami serves the food, except for Marisol, who wants to know if we can get a baby goat so it could play with Pepito. Mami and Leon finish drinking their coffee. Mami gets up from the table and looks out the window again. She's torn her birthday napkin to pieces. Marisol picks up the pieces and drops them into a coffee cup and starts stirring the mess with a spoon.

Leon's calm. "Rome's probably hanging out with his friends in San Juan and lost track of the time."

"We don't even know the names of the boys he works with!"

"There's Carlos," I say.

"Carlos *what*?"

I know Mami is holding back tears, because her nose is getting red.

"Rome and Carlos probably stopped for something to eat, Conci. You're getting hysterical for nothing."

"Maybe you think it's nothing!" Mami starts pacing

and steps on Pepito. He squeals, but she doesn't notice. I pick Pepito up and take him into my bedroom.

"Luz, where are you?"

I walk back to the living room, nervousness like mouse feet running around in my stomach.

"Luz." Mami's eyes hold mine. "Has Rome said anything that made you think he might be doing something secretly?"

The mouse feet are running faster. "I'm . . . not really sure."

Mami surprises me by grabbing my shoulders and holding her face close to mine. "Luz, you must tell me anything you know."

I want to run out of the house, to ride in that car going west with Rome, just ride and be free. Now I know how being trapped feels.

"Mami . . . I don't know *anything* . . . leave me alone." I run to my room and burrow under my blanket. It's dark. And in the darkness, ships are looming like mountains, black water slapping against their sides. Would Rome try to sneak on one to get to New York? I had hammered that worry deep inside me ever since he told me about Carlos's brother stowing away. There's always been a little of the daredevil in Rome. But those monster boats! He might slip . . . the ships might move. . . .

142

I pull the blanket off my head. One of Rome's dresser drawers is partly open. I jump out of bed and stare into the nearly empty drawer. The little mouse feet race. "Mami!" I cry.

Mami runs in and I point to the dresser drawer.

"*Ay Dios mío!*" Her face goes so pale, it scares me.

Leon hurries into the room, carrying Marisol. He sees the opened drawer.

"Luz," he says. "Do you know anything you're not telling us?"

I look into Mami's face and see fear there. My own fear is making my tongue thick. In my ears is the terrible sound of my promise to Rome shattering like a dropped glass.

"Rome . . . told me about Carlos's brother . . . he stowed away on one of the big cruise ships." Mami's hand tightens on mine. "He got to New York that way. . . ."

"Is there anything else, Luz?" Leon asks.

I just stare at him.

"Luz." His eyes bore into me. "Your brother might be in danger."

I can't hold the words back any longer. "Juanita and I saw Rome at the harbor where the cruise ship *La Isabella II* is docked. He made me promise not to tell you."

Leon puts the frightened Marisol on her bed and

takes the car keys out of his pocket. "Conci, I'm going to the harbor. I'll drop you and the girls off at Ana's."

"I'm going with Leon," I say.

"Luz, you come with me!" Mami scoops Marisol up. Pepito's barking. Mami shuts him inside the house as she runs out to the car. I run back and grab him, holding him on my lap as Leon drives to Tía Ana's.

We get there and Mami and Marisol get out of the car. I put Pepito out but I stay in.

"Let Luz come," Leon says. "I'll call as soon as I know something." We speed away with Mami's words "Be careful . . . call me. . . ." trailing after us.

Leon's driving fast. He steers the car easily with one hand even though it shakes every time we go over a bump. He reaches across my lap, opens the glove compartment, and pulls out a chocolate bar. He gives me half. I see at least three other candy bars in the compartment.

"Now you know my secret," he says.

Munching the caramel-and-nut bar helps my heart slow down.

Driving seems to have relaxed Leon. He asks, "Are you still so unhappy about living in Puerto Rico, Luz?"

How much of the truth can I tell him? "Well, not totally."

He takes a bite of the candy bar. So do I. Our munching fills the silence.

"If you could hop a plane to Chicago tomorrow, would you go?"

"Well . . . yes, if Mami and Marisol and Rome went. And you too," I add quickly.

We reach the harbor and I tell Leon which pier Juanita and I were on when we saw Rome. I've finished the candy, but it didn't settle in my stomach right and I feel sick. I have to skip every few steps not to fall behind Leon. He takes my hand. The wind is blowing and I pull the hood of my jacket over my head. The weather is just the way I feel. Awful.

The water is ink black and crests to waves that splash against the huge ships. Darkness makes everything look and sound scary. Our footsteps echo as if we're walking inside a never-ending tunnel. I think we're the only people here, until we see two men standing at the end of the pier near the gangplank of one of the ships.

"Pardon me," Leon says. "Have you seen a boy around here, about sixteen years old?"

One of the men, a cap pulled over his forehead, shakes his head no. The other man puffs out a stream of smoke that hides his face. "Nobody but us out 'ere," he mumbles.

"Those men are spooky," I whisper to Leon as we turn and start back. He answers by holding my hand even tighter.

If Rome climbed aboard one of these monster ships, where would he hide? It's like El Morro here. The ships are the fortress walls locking us out.

The drizzle turns to rain.

"Better button your jacket, Luz."

We reach the steps to the pier and Leon stops and stares at the hulking ships. "No sign of him, Luz." He releases my hand and we head back to the car. I climb into the front seat and Leon slams the doors shut.

"Leon, when Mami sees we haven't found Rome, she'll go crazy."

"Rome thinks only of himself," Leon says angrily.

"It's just that he's so miserable. He's not usually that way."

He starts the car with a jolt, and we travel down the empty rain-slick street. "You're a good sister, Luz," he says.

I sit without talking, scrunched up, inside and out.

When we walk into Tía Ana's house, Mami surprises me. She's worked very hard to calm herself. Though her face has that tight, anxious look, she tells us in a quiet voice that she's called the police and an officer said that they have no news of a sixteen-year-old boy. She told him to look for Rome at the harbor, where *La Isabella II* had been docked. She left Tía Ana's number so they can call if they learn anything about him.

The telephone is like a magnet. We keep looking at it, wanting it to ring and afraid of what we'll find out if it does. Tía Ana and Mami try to keep busy by sorting out Tía Ana's embroidery thread and winding it onto wooden spools. Leon takes apart one of Tía Ana's lamps that isn't working and rewires it. He drops a screw, which I try to find even though he says he has an extra one. Marisol's lucky. She's sleeping. Pepito knows something's wrong. He keeps walking in circles to find the right position to lie down. When he finally does settle, the next minute he's up again.

"Luz, you're sure you don't remember Carlos's last name?" Mami asks me for the hundredth time.

I don't even bother answering.

"Here's the screw," I say, handing it to Leon. It had rolled near the couch and was hidden behind one of Tía Ana's slippers.

The phone rings. I jump.

Leon is closest, but Mami grabs the receiver from him. We freeze in place watching her. I'm saying to myself, please, please, please, let Rome be okay.

"Yes . . . I am his mother. . . . Oh . . . thank God . . .

yes . . . I'm sorry he caused trouble but . . . yes, my husband will come to the station to pick him up. On Caldera . . . yes . . . across from a post office . . . thank you . . . he's leaving now."

Mami looks at us, the receiver still in her hand. "Rome's all right. He's at the station. A policeman picked him up at the harbor."

Tía Ana hugs her, and they both cry and laugh at the same time. Leon takes the dangling receiver from Mami's hand and hangs it up.

I grab Pepito and dance around the room. "Pepito," I sing. "Rome's all right!"

Mami unwinds herself from Tía Ana and throws her arms around Leon. "Oh, Leon. I'm so relieved."

Leon smiles. "Are you going to let go of me so I can get your son?"

We pile into the car again and drop Mami, Marisol, and Pepito at Muddy Blue. I just stay in the car with Leon. He's not in a talking mood, so I keep quiet too.

The police station is easy to find. It's being re-painted, so half of it's light green and the other half is tan. A giant prickly cactus grows by the door, and we steer clear of it as we walk into the station. Rome is slouched in a chair behind a wooden railing. He looks up when he sees us and mumbles hi. One side of his face is scraped and smeared with dirt and blood. His gray duffel is at his feet, and his good black pants are ripped so badly, a long strip is hanging loose.

At one of the desks a policeman is leaning back in a chair, reading a newspaper and drinking coffee. When he looks over his newspaper at us, his eyes are so light, they look blank.

"Officer, this young man is my son," Leon says.

The newspaper hits the desk. The blank eyes stare. "Your son, huh!"

"He's a good boy. It won't happen again."

"It better *not* happen again!" Pale eyes fixes his gaze on Rome, then on Leon. "I should really cage him. He's a wild one. Climbing like a damn chimpanzee."

Leon takes Rome's arm and picks up the duffel. "We'll see to it that he's learned his lesson, Officer. Thank you." He quickly steers Rome through the door and out of the station. I'm so relieved to be outside that my legs wobble.

From my view in the backseat of the car Leon looks as square and immovable as a block of wood. Rome, next to him, is slouched over. I pull off my shoes, lie down, then sit up.

This kind of silence makes me crazy, when people should be talking or yelling and they don't say a word. All the happiness I felt when I first saw Rome has leaked out. I feel like a dropped egg.

Leon pulls into a gas station.

"I'm going to call your mother, Rome. You've given her a night from hell."

Just Rome and me sit in the dark car. His voice seems to be coming from the back of his head. "You told Mami and Leon you saw me at the dock, didn't you, Luz?"

I don't answer.

"Didn't you?"

"I . . . was afraid something awful would happen to you. . . ."

"It did. I didn't make it."

He hunches over and is racked by gulping sobs that sound as if they'll never stop. I want to touch him, say something to make him feel better. But he's very far from me now. There's nothing I can do to bring him closer, to make him know how much I wanted to keep my promise.

When we walk into the house, Mami gives me a quick hug. "Luz, please go straight to bed." She looks at Rome. "You stay here. We've got some talking to do."

"Good night, Luz," Leon says. "Thank you for your company."

Marisol's curled under her covers. She's lucky to sleep through so many troubles!

When I crawl into bed I feel something sharp under the blanket. I turn on the light and glance at Marisol.

She doesn't stir. I pull out a small white box, and when I open it, I find a slip of paper. Under it on a bed of cotton rests a silver coquí pin. I read the note as tears sting my eyes. "This is for you. Tell Mom I'll write as soon as I can. Love, R."

I turn the coquí over in my hand. Rome has left it for me as a good-bye present. But now there's no good-bye. I wipe my eyes with the edge of my blanket. So many tears since I came to P.R. If they were all collected in one place, it could be called Luz Lake.

I study the little coquí. It has the tiniest red line for a mouth. I put it back on its cotton bed and into a carved wooden box I keep under my bed for things I love. The last thing I had put in there was Felipe's drawing of Belleza.

It takes me forever to fall asleep. I don't hear a coquí tonight. I just see a silver one with a tiny red mouth.

The Good-bye Present
That Wasn't

Pepito is so excited to see me when I walk into the house that I can tell he's been alone for a while. There's a note from Mami propped up against the blue bottle of flowers on the kitchen table. I read it once quickly, then again more slowly.

Dear Luz and Rome,

Tata is in the hospital in San Juan. Leon drove Tía Ana, Marisol, and me to see him. He wasn't feeling well and has to take some tests. We may not be home until after dinner, so you should fix something to eat. Do your homework and don't worry about Tata. The doctor said he will be fine. Don't forget to feed Pepito. I love you.

Mami

I don't know what to do with myself. If I were in Chicago I'd say I had the February blahs, but the weather is always so beautiful in Puerto Rico that you can't use it as an excuse. I can't concentrate on my homework. I don't even try. I'm feeling discouraged about school anyway. I'm sure my history teacher wishes I never happened. I thought the last paper I wrote about El Morro was interesting, but she marked *No!* with Halloween-orange ink on all kinds of little stuff like leaving out a comma.

I pull Pepito onto my lap and start to comb him. He hates it and finally manages to wriggle away and escape under my bed.

I show the note to Rome the second he walks in.

"It sounds bad, doesn't it, Rome?"

"Not good." Rome takes a cookie and goes outside to sit under the banana tree. I pour lemonade into two glasses and go outside and sit next to him. He takes a glass and drinks half of it. "Thanks. I was thirsty."

We're so quiet, we can hear each other swallow.

"When you're as old as Tata, going to the hospital is always bad," Rome says, breaking the silence.

"Rome . . ."

He waits.

"The little coquí pin. It's so pretty. But . . . you probably wish you never gave it to me."

Rome finishes the lemonade and rolls the empty glass between his hands.

"If you don't like it, give it to Marisol."

"Oh, but I do like it! I love it."

"So . . . wear it. One of these days it *will* be a good-bye present."

He gets up and walks back into the house. I can't seem to be with Rome anymore without getting upset.

I go into my bedroom, pull my treasure box from under the bed, take the little coquí out, and pin it to my T-shirt. Then I take out the red kerchief Felipe had given me and tie it around my ankle.

I try to get in a comfortable position to read, but as I do, the coquí pin comes loose. Kind of dumb to wear a pin in bed, I think. If I turn over, I could stab myself and bleed to death.

I put the pin back into the box.

One of these days it will be a good-bye present, Rome had said.

When?

The World I Knew Yesterday Is Different Today

It's Saturday and I'm enjoying being lazy and lying in bed. Especially after hearing the good news that the tests showed nothing new was wrong with Tata. Marisol is crawling into bed with me. I pretend that I'm sleeping. She puts her face next to mine and gives me a butterfly kiss with her eyelashes.

"Luz, I picked out a name for my goat! Bobo!"

My eyes fly open. "Bobo! Marisol, that's an awful name."

Marisol's nose goes pink. I'm afraid she's going to cry.

"Well, maybe we can think of a name that sounds a little like Bobo but is prettier. More for a girl."

"Like Baba?" Marisol says hopefully.

"That's the sound a sheep makes, Marisol . . . hey, what about Vida? It means life."

"Vida?" Marisol's not convinced.

"I'm going to call my goat Alegre. That means happy. The two names go together. Alegría—happiness; Vida—life."

Marisol pouts. "I like Alegre better than Vida."

"Okay, call your goat Alegre and mine will be Vida."

"Luz, I know! I'll call her Allie for short!" She jumps off the bed and runs into the living room, yelling, "Mami, we picked the baby goats' names!"

I bury my head under the blanket. It's nice to make a cave of quiet and stay in it for a while, but then Mami surprises me by coming into my room and sitting down on my bed. She has her "I want to have a serious talk with you" look on her face. Her hair is wet from the shower and she has no makeup on. I see some gray hairs that I never saw before. And just last night she had looked up from her book and said that she thinks she needs reading glasses. Is Mami really not young anymore? I want so badly to pull out the gray hairs.

"Luz, we're going to have to have a family talk. Please come into the living room."

Rome is sitting on a kitchen chair and Marisol jumps onto his lap before Pepito does. Leon and I sit on the couch, with Mami facing us on the easy chair.

"I talked to Tata early this morning," Mami says. "He sounded excited. He called to tell us that Ramón and Julio won't be leasing his land or living with him anymore because they're moving in with Ramón's brother, who lives near Ponce. That means Tata will soon have an empty house and he would be happy to have us live with him. Leon would be able to take care of the farm and grow whatever else he wants on the land Ramón won't be using anymore."

We're stunned. Even Marisol is quiet.

"It's a very generous offer," Leon says quietly.

"Rome, Luz, and Marisol, you can each have your own bedroom. There would be a place for Marisol to play, Rome would have a whole shed full of tools—" Mami stops as Rome deposits Marisol on her lap and starts to pace from one end of the living room to the other.

"If I feel off the map *here*. . . ." He holds his hands out, palms up. "What will I feel like at Tata's! You might as well bury me now!"

"There are many things you can do at your grandfather's," Leon says. "Drive the tractor, plant trees, learn how to ride Belleza."

"I don't *want* to ride Belleza!" Rome bellows at

Leon. "Not everybody in the world is dying to ride a horse!"

"We're just exploring possibilities, Rome," Mami says. "Don't shout."

"I'm not shouting!" Rome goes into the kitchen. The refrigerator door groans.

"There's no Coke. Just carrot juice," I say.

The refrigerator door slams.

Mami stands up and takes Marisol's hand. "We all need time to think about Tata's offer. Marisol and I are going to make lunch."

Rome puts the leash on Pepito. "I'm going for a walk. Don't expect me back." The door slams behind him.

Mami watches through the window as Rome stalks down the street. She turns to Leon and smiles sadly. "What did I expect?"

"Conci, Conci." Leon holds Mami close against him for a moment. "I would like to change the world for you."

I think about moving to Tata's all week. It's hard. I don't want to tell Rosita about it, so I feel like I'm keeping a secret from her. I'm washing my teeth when Mami crowds into the bathroom and sits on the closed toilet seat. Now what? I think, then feel guilty for being hard on her when she has so much that worries her.

"I'd like to know what you think about moving to Tata's."

I point to my foamy mouth.

She smiles. "I'll wait."

I try to wash my teeth as long as I can to put off answering her. "Do we have to talk in here?" I ask.

"Of course not. Let's go to my bedroom."

I stretch out on the queen-size bed in her and Leon's white bedroom and sigh with pleasure. "I'd like a bed like this."

"And I'd like an answer to my question."

"About living at Tata's?"

"Yes, about living at Tata's," she says sharply.

"You don't have to snap at me!"

"I'm sorry, Luz, but you're such an expert at distracting me when you want to wriggle out of giving an answer."

"Mami, why are you asking Rome and me what we think of moving to Tata's when you never asked what we thought about moving to Puerto Rico?"

Mami moves closer and smooths my T-shirt over my belly as if it's really important that it has no wrinkles in it.

"I didn't ask you or Rome, Luz, because I was sure you'd say no. Marrying Leon meant marrying his dream, Luz. I believed it was a good dream and it would give us a good life."

Mami isn't looking at me anymore. I can't see her eyes.

"I thought I would be so happy returning to Puerto Rico, Luz, but . . . well, I'm finding it more difficult than I thought it would be. It's been so demoralizing for Leon to have to take terrible jobs until we get our land. There's nowhere for Marisol to play outdoors. I don't see much chance of getting a teaching job. Rome is miserable. I know things have been hard for you. That terrible boy in school who called you . . ."

It's too hard for her to say the word. Rome must have told her what happened.

"Forget him, Mami. He's been transferred to a different school." I change the subject. "Mami, you always act as if things are going just great. . . . I didn't know you were unhappy here."

"I'm not unhappy, Luz. I was just wrong to think I'd be chirping like a bird in spring."

I smile. "A beautiful white bird with long, dark eyelashes."

"I'd be the only bird in Puerto Rico that didn't sing in tune."

"Mami, is there any school around Tata's where you might get a job?"

"Perhaps in the high school. I can't be sure."

"When I think about moving to Tata's, I feel kind of sick. But then, I'm not happy in the school I'm in. I love

Tata's house, and if we don't move, we may be stuck in Muddy Blue forever. And Tata would have to hire strangers to live with him and take care of the farm. I'd worry if they were any good or if Tata liked them. He's not so easy to please, you know."

"Really?" Mami smiles.

"Moving to Tata's would be great for Leon. . . . We won't be as close to Tía Ana though. It would mean I'd hardly ever see Rosita . . . but Rome might like the new school better. And he's always been good at working with machines and tools. . . ."

"We can think of moving to Tata's as an experiment, Luz. If it doesn't work, well, we'll just do something else."

Mami hugs me. Even though I don't fit, I crawl into her lap. She puts her arms around me and starts singing (out of tune):

In Puerto Rico long ago
A little frog said though I know
I am supposed to be a frog
And sit upon a log
I'd rather be a birdie in a tree
And sing ko-keeeee, ko-keeeee . . .

"I've forgotten the rest, Luz. Lucky for you."

"Do you think the coquí's song is happy or sad, Mami?"

161

"It depends on how you're feeling . . . some nights it sounds happy, some nights very sad."

"That's because we don't hear the coquí with our ears. We hear it with our heart."

"Luz, you truly are a ray of light." Mami even manages to hold me on her lap so that my gawky arms and legs don't hang out.

Crazy Uncle

I'm waiting for Rosita on the corner, when I see her running toward me. Something's wrong. There's a purple bruise on her cheek, and her left eye is swollen and dark.

"Rosita! What happened?"

She gasps for breath. "Just tell my teacher I'm sick."

"How did you get hurt?"

A tear squeezes out of her swollen eye. "My mom and my uncle were arguing. He was drunk. I heard him shouting something about drugs. Then I heard a scream, so I ran into the living room and my mother was hunched on the floor. My uncle told me to get out of the house and pushed me so hard, I fell against the lamp. He's sleeping now. He sleeps a lot when he's drunk." She turns and starts running back to her house.

I watch her helplessly. Then I notice the brown convertible parked in front of her house. A light flashes in my brain, and I run to Muddy Blue faster than I've ever run before. Mami's in the kitchen and I grab the phone receiver and push it into her hand. "Mama, you've got to call the police! Rosita's crazy uncle beat her mother. Rosita too. He's drunk. You've got to call before he wakes up."

"*Ay Dios mío!*"

"Mami, call, *please!*"

"Luz. You're sure of what you're saying?"

"Mami, Rosita's mother is *blind*. And he beat her!"

"What's their address?"

I panic. "I don't *know*. Their house is on Regala. . . . It's the only clay-colored one and it has a blue roof. There's a dead palm in front."

Mami dials the emergency police number. Marisol is frightened. I sit on the couch and pull her onto my lap. Mami is telling the police how to get to Rosita's house, when I hear a car. I put Marisol down and race to the window. There's a screech as the brown convertible takes the corner so fast, it looks like it's riding on its side. I strain to see the license number and dash back into the house.

"Mami, don't hang up. The uncle just sped by in his convertible. I think the last three numbers of his license are four–four–five."

Mami quickly tells the police about the car and the license number, than hangs up the phone.

"The police are going right out. Luz, all this must be very frightening to you."

"Mami, please. Can we go over to Rosita's and see how she and her mom are?"

And so, nervousness fluttering in my stomach, I walk with Mami and Marisol, carrying a loaf of bread and a jar of Mami's soup in a basket covered with a red-checked towel embroidered with the words "Home Sweet Home."

Voices in the Bedroom

It was bad luck that Crazy Uncle had packed his stuff and escaped before the police got there. When Mami gives Mrs. Carrera the soup and bread, she holds Mami's hand in hers and presses it to her cheek. She has a bruise on her forehead as if a giant thumbprint with blue paint had been pressed there. Rosita says her mother had a nosebleed. There is a wad of bloody Kleenex on the floor that Rosita picks up quickly.

Fighting squeamishness, I look into Mrs. Carrera's eyes. They are light brown and look perfectly normal until you realize that they stare straight ahead and never move. Her black hair is very long and hangs in a loose braid that reaches her waist. We can tell her back is hurting by the way she's standing. Mami suggests that she rest in bed with a moist heating pad.

"I can take care of her," Rosita says.

Mami looks closely at Rosita's swollen eye. "You rest too, Rosita. Cool compresses may help the swelling go down."

"Rosita and I are good at taking care of each other," Mrs. Carrera says. "But is Rosita's eye bad? Should she be seen by a doctor?"

"It's just swollen a little. It's nothing to worry about."

"Rosita's brave, isn't she, Mami?" I ask after we say good-bye and are on our way home.

"Very brave."

"So is Mrs. Carrera."

"Rosita looked so helpless watching us go," Mami says. "It makes me sad."

I feel the same way.

Of course Marisol couldn't be left out. "I feel sad too," she says.

Today I'm not feeling much better. After school Mami and Leon leave Marisol with me while they drive to San Juan to shop. I teach Marisol how to make stick figures.

She puts all the figures' eyes on the top of their heads. "I like it that way," she insists.

Juanita surprises us by bursting into the house, and giving us each a big hug. "Where's everyone?"

"Mami and Leon are in San Juan. Rome's at his friend Carlos's house."

Marisol hands Juanita her stick-figure drawing. "This is for you," she says proudly.

"Oh, Marisol, thank you." Juanita studies it. "I love your smiling sun. What are these circles on top of the people's heads?"

"Their eyes."

"Yes, of course. Marisol, you've given me my first engagement present." She holds out her hand so we can see the sparkling ring on her finger. "Michael gave it to me last night."

"Oh, Juanita! It's beautiful!"

"You'll have to tell your family the good news, Luz."

"Mami will be so happy!"

"What's engage—" Marisol loses the rest of the word.

"First you get engaged. Then you get married!" Juanita says.

"Can I come to the wedding?"

"I'll tell you when it is as soon as we set the date. I know you have a busy schedule."

"I do," Marisol agrees.

"Will you be moving after you get married?" I ask, dreading the answer.

"That's the hardest part. Even though we'll be only an hour and a half away from my mother, it will seem like the end of the earth to her. The good news is that she had dinner with us last night and she and Michael liked each other instantly."

"She was worried that you were married to your teaching."

"I was, in a way. And then Michael came to the university to give a lecture to the physics department. He sits next to me in the cafeteria. We start talking and . . . well, we haven't stopped yet."

"What if he hadn't been hungry? You never would have met him!"

Juanita's eyes widen. "Scary, isn't it?"

"And if Leon hadn't signed up for Mami's English class, we'd still be in Chicago."

"You still miss Chicago very much, don't you?"

"Yes . . . but it would be hard to think of Mami without Leon now."

"They're good for each other." Juanita looks at her watch. "I have an hour. How about going to the Sun Café to celebrate?"

"Yay!" Marisol cries.

"I'll leave a note for Mami and Leon."

I decide not to tell Juanita about Rosita and her crazy uncle. She's too happy to hear ugly stuff. As far as we know, the police haven't caught Crazy Uncle yet.

We stay in the Sun Café so long that Juanita lets us off at the bridge so she can drive right on to San Juan.

She waves good-bye. "Don't forget to tell Conci and Leon."

She's so happy, I think. Happiness on one side of me, sadness on the other, and I'm squeezed in between.

When we walk into Muddy Blue, we hear Leon and Mami talking in their bedroom with Rome. The door is closed. Marisol runs to open it, and I stop her. "Marisol, let's read for a while."

Marisol gets a book out of her book basket and pulls herself up on the couch, sitting right on Leon's open newspaper. I lift her up, pull the paper out from under her, and drop it on the floor. My eye is caught by a head-line: POLICE BREAK SHOE-SHINE BOY DRUG RING.

My mouth goes dry. I can feel my heart pump. Under the headline are two photographs. One is Crazy Uncle! His name is Arnoldo King Huerto, head of the drug ring. The other photograph . . . I don't want to look at it—is Rome's friend, Carlos Molino, a member of the three-year-old drug ring, who passed drugs to men supposedly stopping for a shoe shine.

I'm terrified to read any further.

"Lula!" wails Marisol. "You said you'd read to me."

"Okay!" I snap. I lift her to my lap and turn to the first page of a picture book about zoo animals. She snuggles close. When my voice begins to slow down because I'm thinking about the newspaper article, she pokes me.

"Lula, read!"

I read. My voice must be monotonous, because Marisol dozes when we're in the middle of her favorite part of the book.

I try, but I can't make out what Mami, Leon, or Rome is saying. I feel like I'm on the edge of a diving board and one little push will send me headfirst into deep water. My right leg is cramped, and when I move it, Marisol wakens and starts to whimper. I manage to pick her up, carry her to her bed, and cover her with her favorite blanket.

She's back asleep. Her face looks so pretty against the light blue pillow. I sit down on the edge of the bed and carefully pull her hand out from under her cheek. I need to hold on to something real, something that won't change in front of my eyes.

Danger!
Vegetable Soup

I lie on my bed, waiting to hear sounds that tell me
Mami is out of the bedroom. I'm too nervous to read or
write. I feel my eyes beginning to close, but I force them
open. Then I hear hammerlike blows. Mami is chop-
ping vegetables, a bad sign. Whenever she's really upset,
she raids the fridge for anything that could possibly be
chopped or sliced to make soup.

I pad into the kitchen barefoot and stand in front of
her. She doesn't lift her head.

"Pepito and I are going for a walk," Leon says. He kisses Mami, but she keeps on slicing.

"Where's Rome, Mami?" I ask.

"He's fallen asleep in our bedroom."

The knife is moving faster. She's on carrots now. I watch the orange circles fall.

"Luz, you'd better go to sleep." She leans over and gives me a quick kiss.

I'm being dismissed. She begins to attack a potato.

"Mami . . ."

"Luz, to sleep. Now!"

But sleep is like a bird, flying near, then swooping away before I can catch it. I try to fill my mind with good thoughts, but they're blacked out by the newspaper-gray faces of Crazy Uncle and Carlos.

I awake when Mami climbs into bed with me. For a minute I think I'm dreaming.

"Luz," she whispers. "Do you think I can squeeze in with you tonight? Rome fell asleep in our room. We didn't want to wake him. Leon's going to sleep in the living room."

I move as close to the edge of the bed as I can and lift my blanket so Mami can get under. Her long hair on the pillow tickles my nose. I rise onto my elbow and look down on her.

"Mami, I'm worried that something awful has happened to Rome."

"You mustn't worry. I do enough of that."

"Mami, I've got to know. Is Rome one of the shoeshine boys in that drug ring?"

Mami freezes. I feel it.

"I saw the newspaper with Carlos's photograph."

Mami looks so pained, I feel guilty.

"Rome did one deal that Carlos set up for him. Carlos told the police nothing about it. We hope he never will."

Marisol stirs and Mami puts her finger over my mouth. "Shhh."

"Did Rome see the newspaper story?" I whisper.

"No. Leon thinks we should show him it to him. It might shock some sense into him."

"Mami . . ."

She focuses her eyes on me. "Yes, Luz."

"Rome wanted to get money for an airplane ticket to Chicago. That's all."

Mami's sigh fills the whole room.

"In Chicago he always said it was stupid to get mixed up with drugs. You remember."

"Leon is very angry with Rome. First trying to stow away, then this. He feels that Rome cares only about himself and doesn't think what his actions do to others."

Mami wipes her eyes though I see no tears. My foot touches hers under the blanket.

"Luz, your feet are freezing!"

"My feet get cold when I think too hard."

"And what are you thinking?"

"So much serious stuff is going on now. Rosita and her mom, Rome . . ."

"Luz, if not for you insisting that I call the police, and being quick enough to get those license numbers, Rosita's uncle might still be free."

She rolls to her side so we're looking straight into each other's eyes. "I thought we would be taking Rome to his real home when we moved to Puerto Rico, Luz. That it would be good for him to go a place that had no memories of your father. It's not worked out that way."

"Mami, one of the reasons Rome didn't want to come to Puerto Rico is that if Dad ever came back, he wouldn't know where to find us."

"How do you know that, Luz?"

"Rome talks to me about his feelings sometimes. The silver saxophone Dad gave him—he won't even let Marisol or me touch it. And when you're not home, he puts on records of Dad playing saxophone. He misses him. That's why he's so mean to Leon."

Mami climbs out of bed and stands, looking out the window. Her hair is as black as the night. A new moon is shining above her head.

"And you, Luz. Do you miss your father?"

I take a long time to answer. "It's more that I miss the chance of ever having him love me."

Mami is still as stone.

"Mami, come back in bed. Please."

She doesn't move.

"Mami, *please.*"

She turns and climbs into bed, and I snuggle close. The only sound is Marisol's breathing.

"Mami, Tata once said that home is the place where all your clothes fit you. Rome told me that he doesn't feel as if he's in his own skin in P.R. Nothing fits."

"Tell me, Luz . . . do any of *your* clothes fit you in P.R.?"

It's time to make Mami smile. "Yes," I say, "my socks."

The Hardest Thing I Had to Do in a Long Time

Rome's been like a robot for days now, doing what he has to with no expression on his face. I catch his eye and he looks away. He's ashamed. I told him I knew he did that drug deal only to get money to fly back to Chicago. He doesn't care what I think.

Mami said she wished he'd forget the whole mess and get on with his life.

"I have no life here," he answered.

It kills Mami when he says that. And then Leon gets mad at Rome for making Mami miserable. And Rome gets mad at Leon for saying he's making Mami miserable. It's not exactly "home sweet home" in the Muddy Blue.

I go to Rosita's house after school. I make a promise to myself not to tell her or anyone about Rome.

Mrs. Carrera is in the backyard, sitting at her outdoor sculpture table. Her red dress hangs below a work apron smudged with clay. The bruise on her forehead has turned a mean yellow and purple, and a large pillow is wedged behind her back. Rosita's father had planted rosebushes near her sculpture table so that she could smell them when she worked. They are the color of a sunset, red and gold. A fringed blue-and-purple umbrella shades her from the sun. So much color! And she can't see any of it.

"Luz," she says, looking toward me with her unmoving doll's eyes. "I'm so glad you've come."

I touch her arm to let her know where I'm standing. I learned this from watching Rosita. "Thank you. My family wants to know how you're doing. And if you give me your grocery list, my mother will be glad to shop for you."

"I will make a list with Rosita's help. That's so nice of her."

"Mama, I want to show Luz the sculptures of me."

She smiles. "Luz will be able to see what a fat baby you were."

I follow Rosita into a long, narrow kitchen with many windows facing out on the yard. The counters have very few things on them.

"My father designed this house," she says. "He made the kitchen long so my mother's cooking things could be in a straight line, always in the same place so she knows right where they are. He put in the windows because on a bright day she can see a hint of light."

"Our counters are jammed. Mami knows where things are but no one else does."

The kitchen leads into a large rose-painted living room with the sculptures of Rosita on black shelves that go across three walls.

Rosita is quiet as I study them. I look quickly past the empty space where the two-year-old Rosita should have been. At age three Rosita is a fat baby, but by five the chubbiness is gone and her hair is in curls that touch her shoulders. At age nine she started wearing glasses. At age ten she had short hair.

"It's like a movie," I say when I reach the thirteen-year-old Rosita, the Rosita I know. "I start at the beginning and watch you grow up."

"I like the baby ones best. The older ones kind of embarrass me."

"It's so hard to believe that your mom sculpted these without *seeing* you."

"She wasn't born blind, so she remembers what things look like. She even remembers colors. She picked out the colors for my room. I'll show you."

Rosita's room is painted bright purple with a white border running along the ceiling and pale green see-through curtains. Her bed is covered with a white quilt that has a pattern of purple butterflies and green and blue leaves. It's on a high wooden platform that has large drawers in it.

"Oh, Rosita! I love it!"

"My father built the bed. I like to be high up." She pulls out a drawer filled with small balls of wool. "This is the wool I weave with on that loom in the corner. It takes me forever to make anything."

"Who taught you?"

"My mother."

"Everything's so neat."

"I have to be neat so my mother can find things."

"You're so good," I say impulsively, making the color rise in her cheeks.

We climb onto her high bed with an armload of books. Rosita says, "Pick any one you want to take home to read. Pick a picture book for Marisol too."

Being in Rosita's room, I forget all about Crazy Uncle and Rome the Robot. It's so safe and private.

When it's time to leave and she points to a door and says that's Crazy Uncle's room, it's like being dropped from a white cloud into a dirty ditch.

"He locked it. We don't have a key."

"Are you going to try to get one?"

"Someday we'll clear it out. My mom would like to move from this house because Crazy Uncle has spoiled it for her. But my father made so many special things. Anyhow, we don't have the money."

I'm about to say good-bye but stop myself.

"Rosita, I've been trying to tell you something for a while, but I keep putting it off."

"Is it bad?" She looks at me anxiously.

I push the words out. "We're going to move to my grandfather's farm."

Rosita's eyes fill with tears.

Our hugs say what we can't put into words.

Down with Grunge

A Thursday in May

Dear Teresa,

It's decided. We're going to live at Tata's house in the country, but we're not moving until school is over. I worry about Rome. He's been getting into some bad trouble here because he's so miserable. He's sure he'll hate it at Tata's. Rosita and I are so sad about being apart that we can't talk about it.

Mami isn't trying to get a job anymore since we're moving. Things have kind of stopped in their tracks.

The only good thing is how Mami enjoys the car Leon fixed up. Sometimes on Saturdays when Leon doesn't need it to go to work, she drives to San Juan and shops or goes to a museum or a bookstore. I went with her last week to a secondhand bookstore and got some fantastic bargains. The books are in Spanish, but that doesn't bother me anymore. We've also driven to see my grandfather. Are you wondering if I saw Felipe? Yes, for about ten minutes. I admit it. I have a crush on him.

You know how you turn your book bag upside down to empty out all the grunge? That's what I'd like to do with my head. Empty out all the grunge! Especially the gross grunge about Rosita's terrible uncle. (That's too awful a story to tell.) But where would I recycle it? It's probably toxic!

Down with grunge!

Your T.F.*
Luz

*Toxic Friend

So That's What a Camel's Face Looks Like

I have been waiting impatiently for Saturday to come. Now it's here and what I wished for is actually happening. Mami, Mrs. Carrera, Rosita, Marisol, and I are sitting on the veranda, talking to Tata on a beautiful May day.

Juanita had told us she was driving to Tata's on Saturday to bring him new medicine. She would be happy to take passengers. Tía Ana couldn't go and Leon and Rome had an appointment to look at some farm equipment. So there was room for Rosita and her mother. We are so happy they came!

So here we are, enjoying the frosty lemonade that Juanita has just served us.

"Tata," Mami says. "Do you mind if Mrs. Carrera looks at your face?"

"Ah, then she will know the truth."

"And what is that?"

"That I look like an old camel."

Mrs. Carrera laughs. "I've always wanted to know what a camel looked like!"

"They have a hump on their back," Marisol says eagerly. "If you go to Chicago you can see them in the zoo." She wrinkles her nose. "Except they're very stinky."

"Tata would enjoy a beautiful woman running her fingers over his face, wouldn't you, Tata," Juanita says.

"Juanita's absolutely right."

Mrs. Carrera looks beautiful in turquoise pants and shirt, a silky royal blue scarf tied around her neck. Her unbraided hair ripples down her back.

Juanita guides Mrs. Carrera to Tata's chair. Tata takes one of her hands and gently lays it on his forehead. We all watch as her wide squarenailed fingers travel carefully over the map of Tata's face, pausing to explore the mountain of his nose, his eyebrow ridges, his chin. Her middle finger returns to carefully trace his eyes, mouth, cheekbones, ears, and once more back to his forehead. One hand cups his head for a moment and then his chin.

"Your voice and your face," Mrs. Carrera says, "go together well."

"Yes," Tata says. "They're both old."

"May I see your hands?"

Tata puts his hands in hers and she holds them, spreads his fingers out, then closes them again.

"This is a nice way to spend the morning," Tata says, winking at me.

Juanita guides Mrs. Carrera back to her chair. "Papi, we've talked to Isabelle about doing a sculpture of your face—a bust—and she said it would give her great pleasure."

"It would be wonderful to have it when—" Mami's words stop.

"When I die," Tata says firmly. "Don't be afraid to say it. It is something I plan to do in the near future."

Juanita kisses Tata on the top of his head. "Papi dear, wouldn't you have liked to have had a sculpture of Nana Socorro's face?"

Tata considers the idea for a minute. "I don't need one. I see her everywhere."

"My mother could make a sculpture of Belleza," Rosita says. "She's very good at sculpting horses."

"Belleza!" Tata exclaims. "Now, that's a fine idea!"

"Papi," Mami says. "We love Belleza, but she's hardly a substitute for you."

"Mrs. Carrera, Belleza has real dignity," Tata says. "Would you enjoy sculpting her?"

"I have a special fondness for horses."

Mami shakes her head at Tata. "Papi, you're incorrigible."

"Perhaps, after you do his horse," Juanita says, "the camel will let you do him also."

"Marisol, Juanita, and Luz, why don't you take Rosita and Mrs. Carrera—" Mami suggests.

Mrs. Carrera interrupts. "Please call me Isabelle."

"Take Isabelle and Rosita to meet Belleza. Felipe rode her this morning. He's probably grooming her now," says Tata.

Rosita's face lights up. "My mother had a horse, Star, when she was little. She made three different sculptures of him. I have one in my room."

Juanita takes Mrs. Carrera's arm.

"Marisol," Mrs. Carrera says. "Would you help show me the way also?"

Marisol, puffed up with self-importance, takes Mrs. Carrera's hand.

Mrs. Carrera lifts it to her cheek. "It's been so long since I held a child's hand."

"If you want, you can make a statue of my hand," Marisol says, excited by her own generosity.

"Thank you, Marisol. We'll have to make plans for that someday."

"Don't you want to come with us, Tata?" I ask.

"I'm fine, *Corazoncito mío*."

I take his hand. "But I want you to come."

"You want to lead the camel?" He pulls himself up from the rocking chair, and with my hand holding his, we slowly follow the others. We catch up to them when they stop to look at Angelina's blue house.

"Can I show Rosita the inside, Tata?" I ask.

He nods and I open the door. "Rosita, come look."

Rosita stands beside me, looking into the sunny room.

"Isn't it perfect, Rosita?"

"Oh . . ." Rosita sighs. She steps closer to her mother. "Mama, the little blue house has wallpaper with hummingbirds sipping from blue morning-glories and the prettiest furniture. It's a house for fairies."

Tata laughs. "My sister Angelina was certainly not a fairy."

Juanita joins in his laughter. "She was more like one of the billy goats gruff."

"Mama, on the desk is a sculpture of the sweetest little donkey."

I hadn't noticed that donkey. I realize that Rosita acts as her mother's eyes.

Perfect timing. Felipe was combing the last tangle out of Belleza's mane.

"Felipe," says Tata, who's a little breathless after our walk. "Our new friends have come to meet you and Belleza."

"Hello, Felipe." Mrs. Carrera holds out her hand. "And this is my daughter, Rosita."

"I'm glad to meet you," Felipe says, shaking Mrs. Carrera's hand. He nods to Rosita, who turns pink.

"Will Belleza mind if I touch her face, Felipe?"

"Belleza is sweet as a marshmallow. She loves being scratched, petted, kissed. . . ."

"And, Mama, Belleza is all white like a marshmallow."

Mrs. Carrera puts her hand on Belleza's forehead, stroking it and drawing her fingers through the silky mane. She rests her cheek against the side of Belleza's face, her arms around the horse's neck. No one speaks, not even Marisol. Mrs. Carrera buries her face in Belleza's mane, and the horse's white hair flows like water over her black hair. She and Belleza are perfectly still for a long, quiet moment. When Mrs. Carrera draws her face out of the veil of white, her cheeks are damp.

Blind eyes can cry, I say to myself. Why not?

"Belleza, you're beautiful and sweet," Mrs. Carrera says as her fingers begin tracing the lines of Belleza's neck. Juanita, wanting to give her privacy, starts talking to Felipe about the sculpture Mrs. Carrera is going to make of Belleza.

"Felipe," Tata says, "wouldn't you agree that Belleza's face is a far better choice than mine?"

"We want Mrs. Carrera to make a sculpture of Tata, but he says no," I say.

"Maybe he wants her to practice on Belleza first." Felipe puts an arm around Tata's shoulders affectionately. "Right, *Compai*?"

"Wrong," Tata says.

"Tata doesn't want a sculpture because he thinks he looks like a camel," Marisol says, giggling. "I think he does too."

Tata pats Marisol on the head and smiles.

"My mother used to have her own horse," Rosita says to Felipe. "He was chestnut brown and had a white star on his forehead."

"Isabelle," Tata says. "Would you like to ride Belleza?

She's very reliable and will give you no surprises. Felipe will ride along on Noche."

"Isabelle, don't let my father talk you into something you don't want to do." Mami holds her finger against her lips as she looks at Tata with an expression that says, "Enough!"

"You'll be safe on Belleza," Felipe says, unaware of Mami's signal to Tata. "Do you want me to help you mount her and see how it feels? I can saddle her for you."

"I don't use a saddle." Mrs. Carrera's hands are traveling along Belleza's back. "It might help with the sculpture if I feel her beneath me."

Felipe looks toward Tata, who nods.

"Okay, then. I'll hold my hands together and you step into them."

Felipe stoops and makes a stirrup of his hands. "I'm ready."

With Rosita guiding her, Mrs. Carrera puts her foot into Felipe's locked hands and flings her other leg over the horse so forcefully that for a panicky second I think she might go over the other side. But she rights herself and sits straight, her hands on the reins.

"It feels wonderful . . . like coming home after a long time away."

"Mama, you *could* ride Belleza," Rosita says. "I just know it."

"Felipe, if you and Noche are willing to escort me . . . I might try to ride a short distance."

"Be back in a minute." Felipe dashes off. Five minutes later he's back, riding Noche.

"Mrs. Carrera, I'll ride alongside you until we get to the road, which is a short distance away. When we get there, I'll ride ahead and Belleza will follow. All you have to do is hold the reins."

"I'm ready, Felipe."

"Belleza, let's go, pretty girl." Felipe picks up the reins.

Both horses start walking. We all stand, watching. Felipe, curly brown hair, white T-shirt; Mrs. Carrera's shining black hair against turquoise; horse tails: white, black; blue sky; green pasture. Rosita grabs my hand and squeezes it. "Oh, Luz!"

If only I could put this moment into a poem!

The two riders reach the road and Felipe and Noche take the lead. Mrs. Carrera's hair and scarf stream behind her in the breeze. We can't hear what Felipe says when he turns to speak to her. It doesn't matter. We can hear her answering laughter.

Not Unless I Want To

Marisol is sound asleep, and I'm in bed reading when Mami comes into my room. What's happening now, I wonder, as she sits on the edge of my bed. Our bedtime talks since we came to Puerto Rico haven't been exactly cheerful.

"Luz . . ." Mami says softly. "I don't like to tell you upsetting things before you go to sleep, but I couldn't find any time to be alone with you today."

I sit up. Tense.

"Leon has persuaded me that Rome should return to

Chicago at the end of the semester, live with Tía Luisa, and graduate with his class next year."

I stare at Mami, feeling as if I've been punched in the stomach.

"Leon's afraid that Rome might get into serious trouble again. Especially with us moving to the country. He's been through this before. With his own brother."

"But . . . then Rome may never live with us again. . . ."

"Except on vacations."

"I mean *really* live."

"No, Luz, he won't." She takes my hand.

"It just won't feel . . . right . . . without Rome."

Her smile is sad. "Luz, do you think it feels 'right' with him now?"

"No. He's like a robot."

"An unhappy robot. Luz, I had a talk with Rome that I should have had a long time ago. About your father." She stops, concerned. "Perhaps we should save this for another day."

"I'm okay," I say, but I'm really not.

"You've had to take in so much lately."

"We all have. Even Marisol," I add, "and Pepito," but she doesn't smile.

"When it became clear that your father had no intention of returning to see you and Rome, I agonized about what to do." She rubs her forehead as if she has a bad headache. "Well . . . I decided it would probably increase the pain if I talked about him as if he were still a part of our life, perhaps feed your hope that he might return. It seemed best to wipe him off the slate for good." She pauses, then picks up again. "When he wrote to tell me he had remarried, I again thought it best not to tell you. I was protecting you. I was protecting myself too, but I didn't admit it." She stands up and walks to the window, then sits down again.

"I don't know if I did the right thing or not. If Rome knew, his secret hoping for his father's return would not have dragged on for so long. He might have been more accepting of Leon." She takes a deep breath. "But who can say? Luz, I told Rome if he ever wanted to contact his father, I would get his Italian address for him. The same goes for you."

I have no words. My heart races.

Mami comes back to my bed, takes my hands, and kisses each palm. "We will never talk about this again unless you want to. Okay?"

I nod.

"Good night. I hope you can fall asleep."

Just as she's about to close the door, I jump out of bed and put my arms around her. "Mami, you and Tata love me enough to make up for . . . well, you know. Dad . . ."

She hugs me tightly and then she's gone.

The Surprise That Really Is

It's Saturday and Leon and Rome are going to the airport to buy Rome's ticket. Rome is so excited, he puts orange juice in his cereal instead of milk.

Leon is drinking coffee with so much cream that it almost looks white. He puts two heaping teaspoons of sugar in too. Mami says it's like a baby formula and she's going to give it to him in a nursing bottle.

Mami's coffee is black as licorice. She seems jumpy. She keeps looking at Leon as if she expects him to say something. But all he does is sip his white coffee.

"Well, Leon? What are you waiting for?"

"You," he says calmly. "It's your idea, Conci."

"But it's your money."

"There is no more 'my' money, Conci. It's 'our' money."

Mami looks at him with love. I don't mind that anymore.

"Luz," he says, "what your mother wants me to tell you is that we will be glad to buy a ticket for you to go to Chicago for two months this summer."

I stare as if he's speaking a language I don't understand.

Rome grabs my spoon and bounces it on my head. "Hey, blockhead. Say something!"

I swallow hard and bring Leon's face into focus. "Two months this summer?"

"Yes. This is all possible because your grandfather is kind enough to share his home with us. I now have free use of the money I had saved to build our home."

I run to Mami and hug her. "Oh, Mami!"

"Hug Leon, not me!"

I've never hugged Leon. He helps me out by hugging me.

That night I call Mami into my bedroom.

"Luz, is something wrong?"

Luckily, Marisol's asleep with KoKo and a purple octopus Tía Ana has just given her.

"I have something to tell you. Come closer."

Her hair falls over my face, soft as feathers. I put my mouth close to her ear. "Mami, I'm glad you married Leon."

Mami's face turns bright as the moon outside our window. She asks me if she can tell Leon what I said.

"Not yet, Mami."

She tucks the blanket under my feet the way I like it. "Sweet dreams."

"I'm going to dream about going to Chicago."

Dear Teresa,

This is the shortest letter I ever wrote. Rome's going back to Chicago to live with Aunt Luisa. I'm coming too, but just for a 2-month visit. Don't go anywhere!

Love,
Luz

But I don't dream about Chicago. I dream that Tata gets sick because all the white flowers in Nana's garden turn black and die. He calls for me because I'm the only one who can bring them alive again, but I don't answer. He calls and calls and gets sicker and sicker.

I wake up. It takes me a moment to realize I've been dreaming.

Night Music

A letter from Teresa! I had given up expecting one a long time ago. The envelope feels pretty thin. Probably one page.

I bring it into my bedroom and settle on my bed.

Short? It takes all of one minute to read! And in a one-page letter she spells Puerto Rico wrong three times.

Dear Luz,

I can't wait to see you but why don't you send me the ticket money and I can come and see you in Perto Rico! Much more is going on in Perto Rico than here. I'm dying for sunshine. We're still waiting for spring and it's the end of May already.

Do you think I am joking about sending me the ticket? I am. But I'm not kidding about wanting to come to Perto Rico. With every day being the same here, there's nothing much to write except that Shanti did quit Wise Girls and the whole club fell to pieces. Hey, guess what! You're not the only one who's going to learn to horseback ride. My grandma gave me a birthday present of a semester of lessons at the stables somewhere in Uptown.

My hand is tired. But I did write a letter, didn't I!

Noodles and oodles of love, Teresa

The letter's a real letdown. I leave it lying on my bed, not even bothering to put it back into its envelope.

We're driving to Tata's for our last visit before Rome and I fly to Chicago. Rome had come into my room while I was getting some of my things together.

"Luz, I worry that I might never see Tata again."

"I worry about that too."

"But you'll be away for only two months."

"Sometimes when Tata's asleep in his chair I'm sure he's stopped breathing and I go and bend over him and listen. I never get over being scared that every day may be his last."

Rome fiddles with the strap of my duffel. "Do you think he's hurt that I'm not staying at the farm?"

"He probably understands. I know he's sad though."

It's not like Rome to hang around unless he has something to say. I wait.

"Luz, did Mami tell you about Dad? That he married again?"

"Yes."

"He might even have another kid or two by now."

I don't answer. He's talking more to himself than to me anyhow.

"Mami said she could get his address for me if I wanted it." He pushes his hand through his hair, forgetting that he's had a haircut and there's nothing much to push through.

"The cruddy way I've treated Leon . . . and at the airport, he smiles and signs a check for hundreds of dollars for my airline ticket."

I just listen.

"Did Mami say the same thing to you about getting Dad's address?"

I nod.

"And what did you say?"

"You probably know."

"Yeah . . . I probably do. Do you still have the silver coquí pin?"

"It's safe in my treasure box. Why?"

"I just wanted to know."

It's a perfect day. The bougainvillea tumbles over the roof of the veranda like a pink waterfall, and the hibiscus bushes around the house are covered with small red trumpets blaring out a happy tune.

The first thing we do when we get to Tata's is eat. Mami unpacks a huge lunch. I set the table on the veranda and Marisol is supposed to be putting paper napkins at each plate, but she tries to fly them like airplanes and lands them in the dirt. "That's okay," she reassures us, and blows the dirt off. I pretend not to see.

Tata rests his hand on Rome's knee. His hands are the youngest part of him, his fingers straight and strong, the moons on his fingernails as clear as ever. Rome looks great with his new haircut. He's even wearing a pair of jeans that are less than a year old.

"Rome," Tata says, "you will be taking driver's education. I hope you keep in mind that driving is not a sport. It's serious business."

"I'll be a lot better than the drivers here!"

"Puerto Ricans can boast excellence in many things, Rome. Driving a car is not one of them."

"It's not cars I'm worried about, Tata, as much as gangs," Mami says as she puts a tomato, corn, and yucca casserole on the table.

Tata looks at Rome solemnly. "My advice is simple. Spend time alone. Face the truth about yourself. Spend time with the trees."

"Driver's ed and tree ed. I got it, Tata."

Rome's so cheerful, I can hardly stand it.

"And, Luz, what is the first thing you're going to do in Chicago?"

"See my friends, I guess."

Rome smacks his lips. "Luz is going to buy a super-deluxe Piero pizza and eat the whole thing herself."

I don't tell him that Felipe's dad's *empanadas* are better than any pizza. I'm saying a little prayer that Felipe will come over. It's complicated though. I wouldn't want to see Felipe when Rome is around.

Lunch is over and Tata has to rest. Leon and Rome go out to check on the mango trees. Mami, Marisol, and I walk upstairs to see who will sleep in which room. There are three bedrooms upstairs and two downstairs. I pick the downstairs bedroom, the one that had been Nana Socorro's sewing room. I like having a door that opens out to the garden. Marisol wails that she can't sleep without me in her room. Mami promises that she can have the dollhouse in her room and pick whatever color curtains and bedspread she wants. That seems to work.

Pepito is close to Tata on the veranda, sleeping peacefully on a green pillow that Tata gave him as a welcome to his new home.

Marisol and I walk out to the goat pen to tell the baby goats their names. They've grown so much since we saw them last. They stand very still, looking at us with those lemon-drop eyes.

"Which one is mine?" Marisol asks.

"You decide."

"That one."

"We should put a different color ribbon around each of their necks so we can tell them apart."

"Allie will have a yellow ribbon," Marisol says. Allie jumps away from Marisol's outstretched hand and runs to Estrellita, sleeping in the shade. Vida follows. They begin running around in circles and then Allie—or is it Vida?—hops onto a big rock. Then Vida—or is it Allie?—jumps onto the rock too, and they start their butting game. I feel awful having to miss two whole months of their growing up.

I brought two giant carrots for Belleza. Marisol gets all excited about feeding her. But when Belleza steps close and puts her muzzle out for the carrot, Marisol squeals and drops it.

"Marisol, Belleza won't eat your hand. Just hold the carrot steady."

"Her mouth tickles," she says, giggling.

I feel more comfortable with Belleza every time I'm with her. She'll forget me in two months for sure. I'll probably have to start from scratch to get her to trust me. I stroke her head and she bends down and nuzzles my pocket.

"She's looking for another carrot!" Marisol cries.

I give it to her and she munches it down.

"That's all I have, Belleza."

I let Marisol help me turn on the hose to fill Belleza's water trough. When Belleza walks over and begins to drink, I try to swallow some of the running water from the hose and get my shirt wet. Marisol grabs the hose and lets the water pour over her head, then turns the hose on me.

"Where's the swimming pool?" Mami asks when we walk into the kitchen dripping water. I mop up, change into the extra clothes I brought, comb my wet hair, and tell Mami I'm going out for a while.

I walk toward Felipe's house without knowing what I'll do when I get there. He told me that I could come and see Noche anytime, and I've been wanting to all day.

Felipe's house is very near, so I walk very slowly. It's white like Tata's, but not as big and doesn't have a veranda. Under a clump of trees I think I see Felipe. He's combing Noche's mane.

This would be a good time to visit Noche and tell Felipe that I'll be going to Chicago for two months and that I'll send him a postcard of the Art Institute.

He moves to comb Noche's other side. How I wish he'd see me and wave, but he doesn't. Disappointed and frustrated, I start to walk back. It would have been the perfect time to say good-bye to Felipe. No, not good-bye. Rosita and I promised never to say good-bye. We say *hasta la vista,* "till we meet again."

As I walk toward Tata's house, I remind myself that it's my house too. My house with my own bedroom and a door leading out to Nana's white garden. Maybe I'll be dramatic like Rosita and paint my room lavender or tangerine. It will be a long time before I live in it though.

Leon and Rome are carrying a basketful of mangoes that they've picked. I run to greet them. Leon is so pleased with how sweet they are that he passes around slices for an appetizer.

"Leon," I say, taking my third slice of mango. "I meant to tell you about the beautiful orchids I saw at the Botanical Garden. You would love them."

He smiles. "The Botanical Garden is a little piece of paradise."

We have mangoes for dessert too, with chocolate chip cookies. After dinner Leon and Rome go to the shed to work on Tata's old yellow tractor.

"It's stiff in the joints like I am," Tata says. "I've thought of going to a body shop, Leon, but they've run out of spare parts for an old model like me."

It's quiet when Leon and Rome leave. Marisol has rocked herself to sleep in the hammock. Mami carries her into the living room and props pillows around her on the couch.

Of course, there are dishes to wash.

"Mami, I'm going to learn what makes a car or tractor work so that I can fix them when they break down."

"No reason why you can't."

"Why don't you learn too? Then you and I can repair the tractor and Leon and Rome can do the dishes."

Mami laughs and puts a bubble of soap on my nose. "My budding feminist!"

By the time we finish it's twilight, and the sky is peach-colored. Tata's reading a book. I swing in the hammock and look at the lacy shadows of the bougainvillea on my bare legs. Mami relaxes in a lounge chair, her book open on her lap. A breeze lifts a page and makes the flame of her reading candle flicker.

"Hmmm, Papi, I can smell Nana's roses in the breeze." Mami inhales the sweet air, rests her head on the chair cushion, and closes her eyes.

I'm not smelling anything. I'm too caught up with an idea that floated into my mind like a seed in the wind.

"Tata?"

"Yes, *Corazoncito.*"

"I've been thinking about Angelina's little blue house."

The breeze lifts a strand of Tata's hair and lets it fall in his eyes. He brushes it away. "Yes?"

"Mrs. Carrera and Rosita might like to move. They don't have much money. They're both small people, so the little blue house would be fine for them."

"Ah, Luz, I'm sorry, but Angelina's niece called to tell me that she would be moving into the blue house sometime in the fall."

"Oh . . ."

"She may change her mind, Luz. She's been known to do that."

"Oh, I hope she does!" I say passionately.

Tata leans back against the chair cushion. "Now, Luz, is there anything else on that busy mind of yours?"

"I don't know. . . ."

"I suspect you do."

"Tata, you're tired. It's okay."

"I'm awake and I'm listening."

"Well . . . if God watches over us, why does he let all those terrible things happen to good people like Mrs. Carrera and Rosita?"

"Ah, I'm very old, *Corazoncito,* and I am still asking that question."

I sigh. "Well, Tata, if you haven't figured out the answer, I never will."

"Think with me a moment, *Corazoncito.* Isn't it more important that we ask that question than find an answer to it?"

"I don't understand, Tata."

"What is more important, *Corazoncito*? That you are given the answer to that question or that you try to help Rosita and her mother find a good house to live in?"

"I'd like them to live in the blue house *and* I'd like the answer to my question. Both!"

Tata holds his arms out, which is his way of saying he wants a hug. I put my arms around him and rest my head against his chest. I feel the slow beat of his heart. Oh, don't stop for a long time, I pray. For a long, long time.

When I straighten up, Tata brushes his hand across my cheek. "I must rest now, *Corazoncito.* Your big questions tax this old mind of mine."

He closes his eyes and leans back on the chair cushion. The breeze blows his hair across his forehead. I comb it back with my fingers and cover him with a light blanket. He opens his eyes just long enough to smile at me.

I walk down the veranda stairs and slip off my sandals. The grass is cool and wet as I wander over to Nana's white rose garden. Resting on the tile bench, I look at the roses and think about Rosita and her mother living in the blue house.

When I walk back to the veranda, Mami stretches and blinks her eyes. She looks at Tata sleeping. I know she's glad that I covered him.

"Are Rome and Leon still working, Luz?"

"Ummm." I settle myself in the hammock and think of Tata's smile as I covered him. It shines in my mind like a star. . . . Felipe and his drawing of Belleza . . . Rosita putting her butterfly barrette in my hair . . . Mrs. Carrera's fingers tracing Tata's face . . . Leon taking out the stones in my knee . . . Juanita and the beautiful things that are real . . . all stars shining in my mind as I look up at the sky.

"Mami," I say so softly that I don't expect her to hear me.

"Yes, Luz."

"Mami, I may not go to Chicago this summer."

I feel rather than see Mami's eyes open wide. "Really, Luz. Why?"

"Well . . . Teresa wrote that the Wise Girls Club fell apart since Shanti left . . . school will be over so I won't see a lot of the kids I like . . . when I really think about it, I don't know what I'll be going back to. And there's a lot here that I don't want to leave. Tata mainly. And you . . . and Marisol and the goats . . . Rosita . . . and I've just begun to make friends with Leon." I don't mention Felipe, but I think of him.

"You still have a little time to make up your mind, Luz."

Two more swings of the hammock. "Mami, if I don't go, can I put the ticket money in my No-Scar Box?"

Mami takes a moment to answer. "I don't see why not, Luz."

"Do you think Leon would mind?"

"I think he'd be pleased."

The coquís have started their serenade. We listen.

"Mami, you know what?"

"What, Luz?"

"I think Rome and Leon are like a little coquí. They need to be in the place they were born to be able to sing."

Two more swings of the hammock.

"And what about you, Luz? Do you think you can learn to sing in Puerto Rico?"

I look up at the stars. They seem brighter the more I look at them. "I'm not sure, Mami. Maybe . . ."

211

We hear voices. Leon and Rome are talking in Nana's garden.

"I won't say anything," Mami says. "If you've decided to stay here, you can tell Leon and Rome yourself."

"I'd rather you tell them, Mami."

"No, Luz. This one is all yours."

Mami's long white skirt catches the light of the moon as she walks toward the voices. The next moment I see her strolling, one arm through Leon's, the other through Rome's. Her two men, I think. Rome is really more man than boy. He's still here in P.R. and I feel a distance between us. What will it be like when he's really gone? I wipe my eyes. More tears in Luz Lake.

Back and forth, I swing . . . the breeze stirs the hibiscus leaves . . . I hear the thrum of the crickets . . . the song of the coquí. . . .

I think of the poem I started to write but couldn't finish. I change it a little.

Under the silver moon
The breeze plays with the flowers
Lacy moon shadows dance on my legs
Tata rocks in his carved wooden chair
Crik, crik, crik.
The ropes of my hammock swish
Ko-keeeeee, sing the tiny tree frogs
Thrum, thrum, hum the million crickets.

The last lines that I struggled for click into place. I say them aloud.

I swing, listening to the music
Tonight I am part of the band.